Probable Paws

(Mystic Notch
Cozy Mystery Series Book 5)

Leighann Dobbs

This is a work of fiction.

None of it is real. All names, places, and events are products of the author's imagination. Any resemblance to real names, places, or events are purely coincidental, and should not be construed as being real.

Probably Paws
Copyright © 2016
Leighann Dobbs
http://www.leighanndobbs.com
All Rights Reserved.

No part of this work may be used or reproduced in any manner, except as allowable under "fair use," without the express written permission of the author.

Cover art by: http://www.tina-adams.com/design

Chapter 1

The somber ambience inside Blake's Funeral Home was a stark contrast to the cheerful spring day outside. Depressing strains of soft music floated out from unseen speakers hidden somewhere in the muted-green wallpapered walls. The cloying smell of dozens of floral arrangements wafted over to tickle my nose, bringing me just to the brink of sneezing.

I glanced longingly at the window. The view was obscured by sheer white drapes, but I knew a bright, sunny day was waiting out there. My attention drifted from the window to the casket in the front of the room.

I hadn't known the deceased well. Adelaide Hamilton had been a friend of my grandmother's, and since Gram had died a few years back, I figured it was only proper for me to attend and pay my respects in her absence. Little had I known that would take up a good part of the morning.

I fidgeted in the hard metal folding chair, resisting the urge to check my watch.

How much longer would this go on?

Up front, Reverend Stone, dressed in a black suit and gray tie, droned on about Adelaide Hamilton, who lay in peaceful repose just behind him. His eulogy included a painfully long account of the elderly woman's life, including how she'd been born in and lived her whole life in our small town of Mystic Notch, nestled in the white mountains of New Hampshire, and had acted as a pillar of society and volunteered at various places, including the historical society and as a school crossing guard.

I decided to amuse myself by watching the family in the front row. Not that a grieving family should be amusing to watch, but this one didn't seem very sad. Probably because Adelaide had been an old lady—her death likely wasn't unexpected. Maybe even merciful if she was ill. Not to mention that they each seemed to have something more important on their minds than the reverend's monotonous eulogy.

The first three seats on the left side of the front row were occupied by three adults whom I figured to be Adelaide's children. They looked to be in their mid- to late-fifties—a little older than me. Gram had been older than Adelaide, and Adelaide hadn't had kids until later in life, so her children would be about that age. I remembered that Adelaide had one son and one daughter. The second woman must have been the daughter-in-law.

The dark-haired woman on the end, who I assumed was her daughter, Josie, sat limply in her seat. Poured in, almost as lifeless as her mother in the casket. I couldn't tell if she'd fallen asleep during the sermon or was on some kind of tranquilizer. Maybe she needed drugs to ease the pain of her mother's death.

Next to her sat a platinum blonde who I assumed was the daughter-in-law, Lisa. I vaguely remembered something about the son's first wife passing away. He must have remarried and, if the cautious looks he kept darting toward the blonde were any indication, *she* was his second wife. She was dressed in designer clothes. A big honking diamond glinted on her left finger, matched in brightness only by the stones that circled her wrist and possibly the shiny, round bald spot on the back of her husband's head. As I watched, she leaned over and whispered in the husband's ear then jabbed a red-tipped finger toward the boy on the other side of him, causing the husband to react like a cowed dog, his head ducking and nodding as he elbowed the boy in the ribs.

The boy, who had been slouched in his chair, sat up a little straighter and glared across his father at the blonde. He looked to be late teens or early twenties. A grandson? He appeared uncomfortable in his suit, constantly tugging the too-short sleeves down over his wrists. He had a cell phone in his hand, which he glanced down at every so often, but his thumbs busily worked the keypad even when he wasn't looking at it.

Next to him sat two girls who I judged to be in their early twenties. I'd come to the wake late and hadn't had a chance to talk to the family, but I'd noticed these two girls right off because of their striking similarities and differences. They had nearly identical facial features, but where one girl was light and bubbly, the other was dark and sullen. The bubbly girl had long mink-colored hair that flowed past her shoulders. The other's was the same color but cropped short. The girls must have been the twin granddaughters I'd heard my grandmother talk about.

Twins ran in the Hamiltons' family, which brought me to the last family member—Adelaide's twin sister, Marion. She was seated in a wheelchair at the very end of the row. They'd removed a chair to make room, but it stuck out into the aisle. She was wrapped in a blond-mink coat despite the warm spring day, and she glowered at the casket like a debutant glowering at bird poop that had just splattered her gown. Or maybe her cranky demeanor just made it look that way. Maybe her glower was genuine grief at her sister's passing. I knew a lot about Adelaide from Gram, as they had been close friends, but I knew practically nothing about Marion. Gram had never mentioned her except in passing.

The dull droning of the reverend's voice had almost lulled me to sleep when I heard a rustle from somewhere behind me. Which was odd, because I was seated in the back row. Maybe someone had come in late and didn't want to make a spectacle of themselves by slipping into one of the empty chairs.

I looked over my shoulder for the rude latecomer. No one was there.

"Pssst..."

I looked again, a jolt of concern running through me as I noticed a swirling mist peeking out from the entrance into the next room. I ignored it. It was probably just glare from the sun, or a mist from the deodorizer plugs I'd seen scattered around, or maybe someone was smoking in the bathroom and the smoke had drifted out.

"Hey ... Willa. Willa Chance."

Shoot. I couldn't ignore my own name. Worse, it seemed I was the only one that had heard it. That, combined with the mist, could mean only one thing. A ghost.

I half turned in my seat, ignoring the dirty look from the lady beside me. Yep. The swirling mist had formed into a human shape. A tiny old lady. I glanced back up front, rising slightly in my seat to get a glimpse into the casket. No surprise there, the ghost was newly deceased Adelaide Hamilton.

"Hey, what are you, blind? I'm talking to you."

I had experience with ghosts and knew there was no point in ignoring them. She'd just continue to pester me until I let her have her say, so I slunk out of my seat and headed into the next room as discreetly as possible.

"What took you so long?" Adelaide, or should I say Adelaide's ghost, glared at me as I pushed her farther into the empty room.

I glanced back to make sure I was out of sight and earshot. "Hi, Adelaide. What can I do for you?" I knew she wanted something. They always did.

"'Bout time you came here." She peered around me, craning her neck to see into the other room. "How's it going in there? Am I getting a good send-off?"

"Reverend Stone is being very ... thorough."

Adelaide snorted. "I doubt my *loving* relatives had any part in that."

"Why do you say that?"

Adelaide misted and swirled anxiously. "I think most of them might be pretty happy I'm gone ... one of them may even have had a hand in it."

"You think one of your relatives killed you, and you want me to find out which one." That didn't surprise me. Ghosts only ever contacted me when they had unfinished business, and usually that unfinished business included seeing their killer brought to justice.

Why they picked on me or how they even knew to come to me, I had no idea. I only knew that a couple of years ago, after a near-fatal accident, they started coming, and they would not leave me alone until I helped them. I was sure Adelaide would be no different.

"Find out which one killed me? No. That's not what I want you to help with."

"Really?" That *did* surprise me. I'd braced myself for a long investigation where I would have to muster up all my skills as a former crime journalist, but if Adelaide didn't want me to find her killer, maybe I would get off easy.

"I need you to find something for me." Adelaide craned her neck to look into the other room again, her face turning concerned. I was vaguely aware that the reverend's voice was no longer droning. The service must be drawing to a close, which meant I didn't have much time to talk to Adelaide. It wouldn't do to have people come wandering in and catch me talking to thin air.

"Money?" I prompted.

Adelaide shook her head. "No. Betty's recipes."

"Recipes?" I wondered if ghosts could be senile.

Adelaide made an odd face. "Surely your grandmother mentioned Betty's recipes?"

Now it was my turn to make an odd face. I'd forgotten, but now that Adelaide reminded me, my grandmother *had* mentioned Betty's recipes. In her will of all places. She'd left explicit instructions that I make sure Betty's recipes go to her neighbor and old friend Elspeth Whipple. I'd looked all over for that darn recipe book but never found it.

"Oh, so *you* had the recipes," I said. "Why would your family kill you over that?"

Adelaide gave an agitated swirl just as I sensed someone in the doorway behind me. I turned to see one of the granddaughters. The dark, sullen one.

"Who are you talking to?" she demanded, her brow creased as she looked into the room beyond me.

"Who, me? No one. I was just looking for the bathroom."

She continued to glare at me suspiciously as I pushed past her to exit the room. "I guess it must be out here."

I glanced back over my shoulder as I walked away down the hall. The girl still stared at me, but Adelaide's ghost was gone. Darn it! I'd hoped she'd stick around long enough to at least tell me where that recipe book was, but I didn't see any sign of her as I elbowed my way through the crowd and out to my car.

I didn't worry about it, though. I knew Adelaide would come back sooner or later. Once a ghost had its sights set on me doing something for them, they tended to bug me until they were satisfied. In the past, that had been extremely annoying, but this one seemed like a slam dunk.

The only thing Adelaide wanted was for me to find some old recipe book. How hard could that be?

Chapter 2

I headed directly to my bookstore after the wake, pausing only briefly to look into the dark windows of *The Tea Shoppe*, the store that my best friend, Pepper St. Onge, owned. Pepper was away visiting her relatives, and I missed our daily chats. She was the only one who knew about my unique ability to see ghosts, and she would've gotten a kick out of hearing Adelaide's request.

In my own store, just a few doors down, I could see my gray cat, Pandora, looking out the window. She was glaring at me with her golden-green eyes, holding my gaze with an ability that seemed almost human. Warning bells rang in my head. Pandora did not like being locked in the store alone, and I did so at my own risk. Usually she expressed her displeasure by leaving unpleasant gifts of hairballs and half-eaten mice. Maybe I'd get off easy this time and would open the door to find that she'd merely clawed up one of the arms of my comfy bookstore chairs.

I unlocked the door and looked in cautiously, my eyes darting around the room for damage. I didn't see any. Pandora trotted over, looking up at me with innocent eyes that flicked from my face to the cabinet where I kept her treats.

"*Meow.*"

I turned the sign on my door to indicate the store was open and gave Pandora a quick pat on her head. "You were a good girl? Okay, I guess you can have some treats."

I grabbed a handful of her favorite salmon-flavored nuggets out of the bag in the cabinet and sank down on the purple microsuede sofa I kept at the front of the shop so browsers could sit and read.

Pandora head-butted my hand, and I fed her a treat.

"*Merowning.*"

"My morning? It was okay. It was a little weird, as I wasn't expecting to see a ghost at a wake, though I guess it is appropriate."

"*Merp.*" Pandora clawed at my hand again, and I absently fed her another treat while I replayed the conversation with Adelaide in my mind.

"*Merooo.*"

I frowned down at Pandora. Sometimes her meows sounded like actual words. I'd inherited her along with the bookstore and the 150-year-old house when my grandmother had died. It was the catalyst for my move back to Mystic Notch, where I'd grown up. A move I'd never regretted and had actually been grateful for. The funny thing was, the more I owned this cat, the more it sounded as if she was actually talking to me. It was almost as if we were reaching some sort of understanding and could communicate with each other without words. No, that sounded crazy. Maybe I missed talking with Pepper more than I realized.

"She did want me to do something, but it was a rather strange request," I said more to myself than the cat.

"*Maraaooo*." Pandora shot a disappointed look at my empty hand.

"She wanted me to give a recipe book to Elspeth."

Pandora remained silent, still eyeing my hand.

"I know. Sounds easy, right? But how am I going to get it, and where do you think she would have stashed it?"

"Probably right in the kitchen."

I swiveled my head in the direction of the voice. Two swirly apparitions floated at the end of the poetry book aisle. A normal person might have been startled to see this, but I wasn't. I was used to them. Along with the cat, the bookstore, and the house, I'd inherited these ghosts. They sort of came with the store. But they weren't just any old ghosts. These two were the ghosts of prominent New Hampshire residents Robert Frost and Franklin Pierce.

You might be wondering how I put up with all these ghosts that seem to flock to me, but Bob and Frank were different. They didn't follow me around. They didn't pester me to solve problems. In fact, they pretty much restricted their activities to inside the bookstore. Sure, sometimes they liked to prank the visitors by pushing books off the shelves, turning pages while they were trying to read, or sending a cold blast of air at someone, but it was all in good fun. And sometimes they were actually good company.

They liked to help me mull over problems. I suspected they were bored and lonely, hanging around in between here and the great beyond with no one for company except Pandora and me. So I usually humored them. Like now.

"The kitchen is an obvious place for recipe books," I admitted. "But Adelaide made it sound like that book might be something she wouldn't keep in an obvious place."

"Maybe she wanted to hide it in plain sight," Robert Frost suggested.

"She said she thought her family members were after it," I said.

Franklin Pearce snorted. "No doubt. Why, I remember my gram treated her recipe book like it was gold. Her cooking was worthy of any White House dinner."

"My aunt had a recipe for buttermilk biscuits that she said she would give out 'over her dead body,'" Robert added.

"*Meow!*" Pandora voiced her agreement as she padded over to the cookbook aisle.

"I guess people do prize their recipes. Even my grandmother left instructions about this very recipe book in her will."

"That seems a little odd," Robert said.

"No odder than leaving me a haunted book store."

"Point taken."

Franklin fixed us both with a look. "Anyway, my grandma used to stash hers all over the house. Under her bed, the library, even in the outhouse. Maybe you should try looking in those places."

"I can't just go skulking around the Hamilton mansion. I need an excuse," I said.

"If Pepper were here, she'd bake up some scones and bring tea over for condolences," Robert said.

"Your gram was close to Adelaide. It would be only proper that you make a personal visit," Franklin added.

"True. And I didn't get to express my condolences to the entire family at the wake..."

Ding!

I looked down at my phone, which was face up on the table. It was a text from my on-again, off-again boyfriend, Eddie Striker, who also happened to be the sheriff in the next county. My own sister, Gus, was the sheriff in this county, but sometimes she had Striker assist on cases. Needless to say, the investigations I did for my otherworldly friends didn't sit well with either of them. Thus, the reason that Striker and I were on-again, off-again. Well, *one* of the reasons. Right now, though, we were on. *Very* much on.

Dinner at your place?

That was it, just four words. Four words that brought a flush to my face and heat to my body. Or maybe that was a hot flash—I was just north of fifty.

Franklin and Robert tittered, exchanging knowing glances. "Is that your young man?"

"Yes." I grabbed the phone and thumbed in my affirmative answer, thoughts of Striker replacing those of Adelaide and her crazy recipe book.

The bells over the door jangled, and two thirty-something women and a young girl entered the shop. Franklin and Robert disappeared. I pushed up from the couch, shooting a friendly, non-salesy greeting at my new customers as I headed behind the counter. Time to get to work. I had a bookstore to run and a dinner date to get ready for. Adelaide's recipe book could wait.

Chapter 3

I closed up shop early, eager to get home and on to my date with Striker. I'd almost forgotten about Adelaide, which could be dangerous. Ghosts were apt to pop up at any moment, and I knew from experience that it was best to be prepared for them. It wouldn't do to jump out of my seat in surprise at a ghost in front of Striker. He had no idea I could talk to ghosts, and I wanted to keep it that way. Most of the time you got a strange reaction if you admitted you talked to dead people, and Striker was such a go-by-the-book kind of guy, he'd probably run off in horror and never talk to me again.

The closer I got to home, the more my thoughts turned to dinner. My cooking skills consisted of Ritz crackers topped with condiments. Striker liked something more filling, so whenever we had dinner at my place it was an unspoken rule that he would bring it. I wondered what it would be this time. Chinese? Pizza? Maybe something from one of the new trendy restaurants that had opened up in the notch.

My stomach grumbled with the thought of all these various dishes as I pulled my Jeep into the driveway of the old Victorian I'd inherited from Gram. Gram had taken good care of the house, but the old farmer's porch alongside the driveway would need a little work this year. Some of the spindles looked as if they were rotting at the bottom. Otherwise the three-story house was in pretty good condition. The white paint was not flaking or peeling, and the black shutters remained straight, with all their slats in alignment. All in all, it was a pretty good house and had a lot of wonderful memories.

I opened the driver's door, and Pandora shot across the console, digging her razor-sharp claws painfully into my thighs as she used them as a springboard to leap out of the car.

"Ouch!" I rubbed my legs and scowled at the cat, who trotted over to the edge of the woods as if she were heading out for a leisurely night of mouse hunting.

"Not tonight, Pandora." Though I knew the cat could take care of herself, I worried about her being out in the woods at night. There were predators here in the notch, and I didn't want her to get hurt.

"*Spethhhh,*" she hissed, plunking her bottom down at the edge of the path that led to Elspeth's house and staring at me like a petulant child.

My eyes flicked to the woods behind her. It was still light out and would be for another hour or so, and I had a couple of hours before Striker would be over. Maybe visiting Elspeth wasn't such a bad idea.

Pandora had been cooped up inside all day, and I could tell she wanted to stretch her legs. A little journey through the woods would probably do her good, and Elspeth had a gaggle of cats that Pandora liked to hang around with. Not to mention that if I let Pandora get a little exercise and some "cat time," she'd be less needy and more apt to leave Striker and I to our own devices later on.

"Okay, but just a short visit." I dropped my tote bag on the porch and jogged toward the path. Pandora ran off ahead of me, slowing up a bit once she got deeper in the woods so that I could catch up. We walked side by side, as was our usual custom. It always amused me that she stuck right beside me like a dog. Almost as if she were protecting me from something in the woods.

There wasn't really anything to be protected from in there, though. The woods were friendly, almost magical. The path to Elspeth's house was well worn, and I could practically travel it with my eyes closed. Even though she lived a few streets over, I'd taken this shortcut to her house my whole life. First with Gram and one of her many cats by my side, and now with Pandora.

In a way I'd inherited Elspeth along with everything else. Gram and Elspeth had been friends since they were little girls. I had fond childhood memories of Elspeth along with the memories of my grandmother. One of Gram's final wishes was that I check in on the elderly lady to make sure that she was getting along. From what I could tell, Elspeth was healthy and spry, fully capable of taking care of things on her own, but I checked in anyway to honor Gram's wish. Plus, I liked her company.

I picked up the pace, hoping to generate some warmth. A slight chill had developed in the air, as it does on spring nights in the mountains, but the day had been warm, and I hadn't thought to put on my usual navy-blue hoodie. The sun was still up, slanting mystical, diffused light through the trees. The oaks, birches, and pines cast enchanting shadows, which added to the forest's magical feel. A childlike, spellbound feeling bloomed in the middle of my chest—a feeling that often came to me on the way over to Elspeth's house.

The woods were peaceful but at the same time alive with the twittering of chickadees, sparrows, and nuthatches. The canopy of overhead leaves fluttered in the slight breeze, causing dots of sun to dance on the path. The squirrels and chipmunks rustled softly in the brush on the sides of the path. When I was a little girl I'd fantasized that Elspeth was a magical witch. The fantasy was probably brought on by my journeys through the woods with Gram and intensified by the fact that Elspeth's green-and-pink turn-of-the-century Victorian with fancy gingerbread molding at the end of the path looked as if it came straight from a Grimm's fairytale book.

The scent of baking cookies hit me seconds before that fairytale house came into view. It grew stronger and even more delicious as I approached the house, with its rose-covered wrap-around porch. The thorny rose vines that twined around the spindles and railings were just starting to bud. In another week, they would be in full bloom, creating a blanket of fragrant pink flowers that obliterated the railing itself.

Elspeth must have taken the white porch rockers that we often occupied on hot summer nights out of storage. Her orange-and-white cat, Tigger, sat in one of them, his tail twitching and keen eyes watching us approach almost as if he'd been waiting for us.

Pandora trotted onto the porch, and the two cats sniffed out a greeting as I knocked on the door.

"Come in!" Elspeth yelled from the kitchen.

I open the door wide enough for Pandora to slip in, but she just shot me a disdainful look and then trotted off with Tigger toward the barn, where the rest of the cats hung out. Nothing unusual there—Pandora often preferred feline company to human.

I walked through the living room, which was decorated in dark mahogany antiques, and down the hall to Elspeth's cheery, old-fashioned kitchen. She was just sliding a cookie sheet out of the oven and turned to greet me. Her cheeks were flushed, wisps of snow-white hair escaped the braid that wound around the top of her head, and her blue eyes sparkled.

"You're just in time to taste-test these spritz cookies. My grandmother used to make them." She slid each golden cookie onto a cooling rack with a spatula.

"Great. I'm starving." I sat at the table while she grabbed a plate from the cabinet and then put several cookies on it.

"Milk?" Her hand hesitated over the knob of the cabinet where she kept the glasses.

"Please."

She poured milk into a delicate pink Depression-glass tumbler and placed it along with the cookies on the table in front of me. "I hope they taste okay. I'm getting older, you know, and my memory for ingredients isn't the same."

I was already biting into the cookie, which was sugary, buttery, and delicious. I waved my hand. "Get out. You're not getting any older. These are fabulous."

Elspeth beamed with appreciation. "Oh, that's good. You know it does get harder to remember, especially without my recipe book."

Recipe book? What an odd coincidence that Elspeth would mention a recipe book ... or was it?

"You know, Gram mentioned a recipe book that she wanted to give to you. Betty's recipes? Who is Betty?" I didn't dare tell her I'd heard about the recipe book from Adelaide as well. It would likely scare the wits out of her if she thought I talked to ghosts.

Elspeth busied herself with the cookies on the counter, her back to me. "Oh, yes. Betty was a friend of ours. She did have the best recipes." She turned and looked at me intently. "And you have the recipe book?"

"No, that's the thing. I looked in Gram's things, but I never found it." I shrugged, trying to act nonchalant. "I think she mentioned something about Adelaide Hamilton."

Elspeth's gaze intensified. "Adelaide? Adelaide just died."

"I know. Were you friends with her?"

"A long time ago. Not so much lately. Her family didn't let her get out much." Elspeth pursed her lips in disapproval.

"Gram might have given her the recipe book. I wonder if she still has it and where she might keep it."

"If she did have it, I'd say she'd keep it from that vulturous family of hers. They don't appreciate anything. And certainly not good recipes." I thought I saw a dark flicker in Elspeth's eyes, but then her face cracked into a smile, and she laughed. "Silly me. It's just recipes. But if you did happen across that book—the one with Betty's recipes—I would dearly love to have them."

"Sure. I'll keep my eyes peeled."

"Well, that's enough about that." She nodded at my empty plate. I'd already scarfed the last cookie and was happily chewing. "If you think those are good enough, I'll pack them up to bring them over to Emma for the church bake sale."

"They're delicious." I brought the plate and glass to the sink.

"Oh, don't worry about those." Elspeth took the dirty dishes out of my hands. "I'll take care of them. You better rush home. Don't you have a date with that nice young man tonight?"

"Yes, I do. How did you know?"

"Oh, just a lucky guess." Elspeth ushered me out of the kitchen, walking me to the front door and leaning out as I walked down the porch steps. "If Adelaide still had that recipe book, I bet she had it stashed away somewhere special. Betty handwrote those recipes, and there's not another one like it. Could be in the last place you might think to look ... of course, that might just be another lucky guess."

"I'll keep that in mind." I jogged down the steps and over to the woods, looking for signs of Pandora. She was probably still in the barn, and I didn't have time to wait for her. She could find her way home easily enough.

As I started into the woods, I looked back at the house. Elspeth had gone back inside. Funny how she'd known I had a date with Striker. Of course, it was no secret that we saw each other frequently, but something niggled at me. Elspeth was uncannily perceptive and seemed to know a lot of things before you even mentioned them. Which made me wonder if Elspeth's guesses were more than just lucky.

Chapter 4

Pandora followed Tigger into the barn, as she had many times before. Even though the sun still had yet to set, the inside of the barn was dark like twilight, the only source of light filtering in from the thin crack between the sliding doors. Pairs of curious green, gold, and blue eyes blinked at her.

"To what do we owe this honor?" Inkspot, a large black cat, peered over the side of the loft, his brilliant-green eyes sparked with inquisitive interest.

"I've heard tell of an important book that I believe interests us." Pandora sat in the middle of the barn. Cats slunk their way toward her from the dark shadows. Inkspot leaped down, landing softly on all fours in front of her.

"You don't say? What kind of book?" Sasha, a sleek Siamese, rubbed her silky white cheek on one of the stall doors.

"A recipe book."

"Recipes?" Otis, the rare male calico, scoffed. "For kibble, I hope."

Otis's words set off a titter of meows amongst the other cats. Pandora's whiskers twitched in anger. There was no love lost between her and the fat calico. He thought himself superior, as he was a rarity since only three percent of calicos are male. The two of them had gotten along as if they were oil and water from the get-go. He was of the old ways, and she was of the new ways. Their constant clashing had been a source of exasperation for Pandora until recent events had forced Otis's hand, and he had shown that deep down in his soul, he was not as bad as he pretended to be on the outside.

She'd thought those events had forged an understanding between them ... a truce of sorts, but his words cut deep. She turned to look at him, her anger dissipating as she noticed a teasing smile cross his lips before he turned away. Apparently old habits die hard.

Pandora ignored him. "The ghost of Adelaide Hamilton has enlisted my human's aid."

That got their attention. They were an elite species of cats sworn to help humans since ancient times—a task made more difficult by the fact that humans simply didn't have the felines' superior methods of communication. When a ghost contacted humans for help with a physical item, it was something to take notice of.

"Her help? For what?" Kelley, a Maine Coon, flicked her fluffy tail as she strode into the circle that was now forming around Pandora.

"To find this recipe book."

"How could a recipe book be of importance?" Otis peered down at them from his perch on top of a stack of hay bales.

"She says it should be given to Elspeth for safekeeping." Pandora smiled at the other cat's hissing intake of breath. She had saved this morsel of information so she could impart it when it would have the most impact. The cats knew that Elspeth was one of the revered ones and anything that named her specifically was of great importance.

Hope, the young chimera cat whose face was divided into two colors equally straight down her nose—one side black and one orange—padded over to sit beside Pandora. "We should take heed. I hear there is someone evil in Adelaide's circle."

"Someone who would have this recipe book in the wrong hands, then?" Sasha asked.

"Most likely," Hope said.

"Then we must figure out how to help the humans find this book," Inkspot's deep baritone rumbled with authority.

"And protect your human from this evil one," Hope added.

"Yes, but is your human willing to help? She has been...reluctant in the past," Otis asked Pandora.

The hair on Pandora's back prickled with indignation. "I'm training her well. She'll help."

But would she? Pandora wasn't sure. Willa had no idea of the value of the book, and from what she'd said in the bookstore, it had sounded as if she didn't attach much importance to the task. Hopefully Adelaide's ghost would keep her on track.

"Well then, Pandora, what are you waiting for?" Inkspot asked. "Go home and set your human in motion."

***

Pandora trotted out of the barn and sniffed once toward the house. As she suspected, Willa was no longer there. It wasn't unusual for Willa to head home without her, so she hurried down the path, ignoring the tasty chipmunks that scurried through the underbrush trying to collect that one last morsel before sunset. Willa would have a more delectable treat in her cat bowl at home.

As she drew near the house, her heightened senses picked up the scent of Chinese food and Striker. Her mouth watered. Maybe she would get a little shrimp and lobster sauce in her bowl tonight. But her happy thoughts about dinner faded as she felt the sharp prickle of agitation in the air. Striker was upset about something.

She burst out of the woods and immediately saw what was causing the agitation. Striker was being accosted by a ghost, and he didn't look happy about it. Her whiskers twitched in amusement as she padded over to them.

It was funny that both Striker and Willa saw ghosts. But not the same ghosts. They were each tuned in to different planes, therefore the ghosts that Striker could see were invisible to Willa and the ghosts that Willa could see were invisible to Striker. To make matters even more entertaining, neither one of them wanted to admit to the other that they had this ability. Pandora could see ghosts on all planes, and so she found both Willa and Striker's behavior—when they were trying not to let on that a ghost was present in each other's company—quite comical.

The ghost was a man dressed in 1950s attire. It was evident that Striker was trying to get rid of the apparition, though he was making a valiant effort of hiding this fact by pretending he was busy hauling the take-out food from the back seat of his sheriff-department-issue ten-year-old Crown Victoria.

"Not now." Striker made shooing motions at the ghost.

The ghost huffed and swirled, leaving droplets of ectoplasmic mist on the grass. "I don't work on your schedule, boy."

"Fine. What do you want?" Striker rearranged the white take-out containers inside the bag.

"A fine attitude you have when someone comes asking for your help. Did your mother teach you those manners?"

"Look, I'm sorry, but I'm kind of pressed for time. I have a date, and if she sees me talking to thin air..."

"I'll get to the point, then. I'm Louis Hamilton." The ghost paused for effect. An effect that was apparently lost on Striker, but not on Pandora. Hamilton? Must be related to Adelaide and possibly to the important task Adelaide had bestowed on Willa. Maybe it would be easier than Pandora had first thought to recover the recipe book. With Striker working it from one side and Willa from the other, it should be a piece of cake.

"Nice to meet you, Louis. How can I help?" Striker's tone was reluctant, his eyes darting to the farmer's porch to make sure Willa wouldn't catch him.

"You don't know who I am?" Louis was taken aback.

"Should I?"

"I'm the husband of Adelaide Hamilton, who just died on Tuesday."

"My condolences...or is it congratulations?"

"It would be congratulations, if I were reunited with her. But there's something keeping us apart. I've been waiting for decades for her to pass over so we could see each other again." Pandora's heart clenched at Louis's heartsick tone.

"I don't know how to help with that." Striker piled duck sauce on top of the take-out boxes.

"I do. There's a book. Betty's Recipes, she called it. If you find that book, I just know we'll be reunited again."

"Mewit!" Pandora couldn't help but let her excited meow squeak out. Both Striker and Louis frowned down at her then turned their attention back to each other.

"That seems a little far-fetched," Striker said. *"A recipe book? How do you know it'll help? And just what am I supposed to do with it?"*

"I don't know. Not everything is revealed to us here in the afterlife, you know. Just bits and pieces. But one thing I know is that you have to find that book!" Louis swirled in agitation.

"Okay, calm down. I'll help if I can, but just where am I supposed to look for it?"

"Well, if I knew that, I wouldn't really need a detective, would I? All I can say is she would have kept it near to her ..." Louis's voice faded as his misty figure dissolved into droplets that fell to the ground.

Striker straightened, the take-out bag in his hand. He rubbed his forehead and sighed, muttering under his breath. "Damn ghosts. You'd better not come back during my date, old man. I'll go to the afterlife just to kill you again."

Striker cast a furrowed-brow glance at Pandora. "What are you looking at?"

"Mew!" Pandora trotted off toward the house, satisfaction bursting in her chest. She didn't break stride as she slipped in through the cat door. Running past the living room, she only gave a cursory glance at the round glass paperweight on the coffee table. It had been a gift from Elspeth when Willa first moved here. Little did Willa know that the seemingly innocent paperweight could contain vitally important images. But tonight, no images were inside it, so she continued upstairs to Willa's bedroom, where her human was in a pitched battle with her unruly copper curls.

Pandora jumped up onto the dresser beside Willa, sat on her haunches, and proceeded to clean her face with slow, dainty movements. She focused hard on looking cute, hoping her cuteness would prompt Willa into dumping some of the Chinese shrimp she could still smell wafting in through the open window into her cat food bowl.

While Willa struggled with her hair, Pandora sighed with contentment. Retrieving the recipe book was going to be easier than she thought. With Striker on the case and Adelaide's and Louis's ghosts pushing things along, Pandora's job was practically done for her.

Chapter 5

"Dammit!" I tugged at my red curls, hoping to tame them into unified corkscrew spirals, but no matter what I did they ended up springing into a messy bird's nest.

"I don't know why I bother," I said to Pandora, who was sitting on the bureau, washing her face as if she hadn't a care in the world.

"Food's here!" Striker's voice called out from the kitchen, jerking my attention back to the mirror. Shoot! I wasn't ready. I made one last attempt with my hair then grabbed my mascara and swiped a few lashes. That would have to do.

Pandora leaped off the bureau and beat me to the kitchen, where Striker already had the white containers open. Their spicy fragrance drifted toward me, making my stomach pinch. He turned from the cupboard, where he was pulling out dinner plates. His gray eyes lit up in a genuine smile that crinkled at the edges and melted my heart.

"You look great," he said, his deep voice inducing more melting, but now of other places besides just my heart.

"Thanks. You do, too." My pulse kicked up a notch. Striker was wearing a plain gray T-shirt, which would have been uninteresting on anyone else. But the way his broad shoulders and muscular chest filled it out made it very interesting indeed. We stared at each other for a few magical seconds before the moment was broken by Pandora's annoying meow.

She was sitting beside her cat bowl, looking pointedly from the empty bowl to the Chinese food boxes on the counter and then back again.

"I get it. You want lobster, right?" I said.

"Meow!"

I picked a few juicy lobster morsels out of one of the dishes, wiped off the sauce, and dropped them in her bowl. Pandora immediately focused her attention on the lobster and ignored Striker and me as we filled up our plates and sat down at my table. I was happy to see Striker had already filled two crystal glasses with wine.

We dug into our food. I had jumbo shrimp and crab Rangoon, which I dipped into the duck sauce. Sweet, tangy, and crunchy, my three favorite factors in food. Striker got to work on a big plate of beef and broccoli. We chatted about our day. I was careful to avoid any mention of Adelaide Hamilton for fear of conjuring up her ghost.

Not mentioning Adelaide didn't work, though, and right in the middle of my second jumbo fried shrimp I saw the wispy beginnings of a ghost forming.

"Psst..."

Adelaide hovered by the refrigerator, posturing and gesturing to get my attention. I shifted in my seat so as not to look at her directly and did my best to ignore her. Maybe she would go away.

"Is something wrong?" Striker raised a brow but kept munching.

"No. The food is delicious." I beamed a reassuring smile.

"Over here!" Adelaide floated over behind Striker. "Are you blind?"

I closed my eyes and tried to telepathically wish Adelaide away.

I might have said something out loud, because Striker asked, "Did you say something?"

"Yes. I asked how the rice was." Covering for myself quite cleverly, I thought.

I didn't dare look directly at Adelaide, but I could see her put her hands on her hips and make an annoyed face out of the corner of my eye. She floated over to the table next to me, and my anxiety levels escalated. I didn't have a good feeling about what she was about to do.

Her ghostly hand snaked out toward my wine glass, brushing against my arm as it tapped the glass, moving it slightly. I felt a cold chill. Did Striker feel it? Had he seen the glass move? I glanced up at him, but he was focused on his food. The glass moved again, this time making a scratching sound on the table.

Striker looked up, and I grabbed the stem to cover the movement. "This wine is good."

"Moscato. Your favorite." Striker flashed me one of his charming smiles, but I was too chilled from Adelaide to melt this time. The fact that he remembered my favorite wine did earn him points, but I was too distracted by the tug-of-war on my wine glass to think much about it.

The glass was growing incredibly cold, and I noticed a thin sheet of ice starting to form on the wine. A freezing pain shot to my fingers. I jerked my hand away, and the glass flew off the table, splashing wine all over my new lavender silk shirt before smashing to a million pieces on the floor.

"Shoot!"

"You okay?" Striker looked concerned.

"Yes. Fine. My shirt might not be. I better go see if I can save it." I glared at Adelaide on my way to the bathroom.

"I'll clean this up for you," Striker called after me.

Adelaide followed me into the bathroom, and I slammed the door shut, whirling on her. "Just what do you think you're doing?" I hissed.

"I had to do it. You weren't listening to me," Adelaide said.

"Did it ever occur to you that I was on a date and this could wait until the morning?"

"No, and besides, don't be selfish. *You're* on a nice date, and my Louis might be lost to me forever."

I dabbed at my shirt with a facecloth and wondered if I should use water. Silk and water do not get along, but it was already wet with wine. "Louis is your husband?"

Adelaide nodded. "He died forty years ago. I never remarried, you know. Loved him too much. I always thought that when I passed, he'd be here waiting for me."

I kept scrubbing. Maybe I should turn the hair dryer on it. "He isn't?"

"I can't find him anywhere. I've run into old friends, family. Not Louis."

The scratchy tone in her voice stole my attention from the wine stain. Was she crying? I looked up to see that her face was all puckered. My heart clenched. I didn't even know ghosts could cry.

"I guess he didn't wait for me ..." A sky-blue tear slid down her misty face.

"Ohh ... don't cry. Are you sure you've looked everywhere?" I dropped the facecloth and tried to pat her shoulder in a comforting gesture, but my hand slid right through her. I pulled it back quickly, holding it to my chest. It was half frozen.

Adelaide was unconcerned about my wounded hand. "Well, that's the thing. I'm in a holding pattern. A limbo of sorts. I can't see all that is beyond because I have unfinished business."

"The recipe book?"

"Yes, please find it, Willa ... you're my only hope." Her tone was desperate.

Ugh... I hated being someone's only hope, even if that someone was a ghost. "Fine. Where do I look?"

Adelaide turned around suddenly, her face scrunching in dismay. She started to fade like a snowy television station. She spoke, but her words were distorted. I thought she said something about Daisy.

"Daisy? Adelaide, stick with me," I begged.

"Can't. Gotta run ... but I'll leave you with a warning. Watch out for my family... some of them cannot be trusted."

"Which ones?" I yelled, but too late. She was gone.

I finished drying my shirt and returned to the kitchen to see Pandora batting at something as if she were playing with an invisible friend. I was afraid Adelaide had appeared back in the kitchen, but as I turned the corner I was relieved to see nothing but thin air.

" ... me alone." I caught the tail end of Striker whispering to Pandora.

"Are you talking to Pandora?" It was odd because while his head was turned in her direction, it appeared that he was looking at a spot several feet above the cat.

Striker whipped his head around. "Huh? Yes. Pandora. I was talking to Pandora. She's acting crazy."

My eyes dropped to Pandora sitting on the floor with what looked like a smirk on her face. She made a little meowing noise that sounded almost like a chuckle then stood and turned her back, flicking her tail as she sauntered out of the room. She was starting to act more and more like a person every day.

I sat back at the table. Striker had cleaned up the mess from the shattered wine glass and poured me another. I picked it up and inclined it toward him. "Thanks."

"You're welcome." His smile was a little tight, not as charming as usual, and there was something wary in his eyes. I silently cursed Adelaide.

She'd made me act funny, and now Striker was probably regretting coming over in the first place.

We finished and cleaned up, but the damage was done. Striker was acting distracted. I was on constant lookout for Adelaide's ghost, and my leg was throbbing. Though almost healed from an old car accident, my leg still hurt when I got stressed. I guess Adelaide's ghost had affected me more than I'd thought. I grabbed the tube of *Iced Fire* from the basket on my counter then sat at the table and hiked up my pant leg, massaging the pungent peppermint salve into my leg.

"Leg hurt?" Striker asked.

I nodded.

"Let me do that."

Striker poured me another wine and pulled a chair up in front of me then picked my leg up gently and placed it in his lap. Soon his massage and the wine were doing their trick. I hadn't seen a wisp of a ghost in over an hour, and I was feeling a lot more relaxed. When his capable fingers worked their way up my leg, I started to feel hopeful that the night could be salvaged after all. I could tell by the look in Striker's eye that he was having the same thoughts.

And now I was more determined than ever to find that stupid recipe book so I could get rid of

Adelaide before she ruined too many more of my evenings with Striker.

Chapter 6

The next morning I was in good spirits as Pandora and I trotted toward *Last Chance Books*. Down the street, the dark windows of Pepper's Tea Shoppe brought on a pang of loneliness for my friend. I would love to bend her ear about Adelaide's recipe book and my date with Striker. Though the date had ended well, I still sensed that Striker had something on his mind. Then again, if I mentioned that to Pepper, she'd probably try to fix it with one of her teas, which she fancied had magical properties. My jury was still out on whether or not the teas could "make things happen." The one time she tried to use her tea to bring Striker and I together had not gone as planned.

The bookstore regulars, Bing, Josiah, and twin sisters Hattie and Cordelia, were already lined up outside the front door. I'd inherited the quartet of senior citizens along with the bookshop. They'd been meeting at the bookstore first thing in the morning with Gram to gossip about town events for over forty years. Who was I to stop a tradition like that? Besides, I liked their company, and they brought the coffee.

We'd missed our meeting the day before, as Adelaide's service had taken precedence. Since I'd gotten to her service late, I hadn't had a chance to do much except for nod a greeting at Bing. Hattie and Cordelia had been there, too, dressed in matching burgundy polyester pantsuits. I hadn't seen Josiah, though. Maybe he didn't attend. Maybe one of them would have some insight as to where I could find this Daisy person Adelaide had mentioned.

"Morning, everyone!" They returned my cheerful greeting, moving aside to let me unlock the big oak door that was the entrance to my bookstore. I opened it and gestured for them to enter ahead of me. Bing, last in line, handed me a Styrofoam cup as he brushed past. I flipped the little plastic tab, watching the steam curl out of the top as I let it cool before sipping. Pandora rubbed against Bing's ankles, then after he obliged her by bending down and scratching her behind the ears, she hopped up into her plush cat bed in the large storefront window and snuggled in for the day. The others took their places on the purple microsuede sofa and chairs.

"Such a shame about Adelaide." Hattie opened the conversation.

"Indeed." Bing nodded and swiveled his head to look at me. "You left the service suddenly yesterday. Were you feeling ill?"

"No. I just had to get back to the store." I looked down at the rim of my coffee cup, my cheeks burning at the lie. I was no good at lying.

"It's a shame she died so young." Cordelia glanced at me out of the corner of her eye. "And maybe not naturally."

Josiah leaned forward, elbows on thighs, with his Styrofoam cup cradled in both hands. He scowled at Cordelia. "Now, what are you going on about? She was eighty-something, and I heard she had cancer."

Cordelia shrugged. "Eighty-something is young. And besides, her doctor said she was putting up a good fight. She was in remission."

"You think her death wasn't natural?" I asked.

"Well, it did seem kind of sudden," Hattie said. "We just saw her down at the *Cut and Curl* last week, and she was getting a new permanent. Does that sound like someone who's dying?"

"What does Gus think?" Cordelia asked me.

"I don't know. I don't think there's an investigation, so she must think it was natural." I hadn't seen my sister, Gus, at the service. Maybe she didn't feel as if she had to keep up Gram's obligations as I did, or maybe she was busy working.

Her job as sheriff kept her busy. Either way, if she had suspected foul play, she would have been at the service. My mind flew back to Adelaide's suspicions that someone in her family had done her in. But that wasn't really *my* problem. *My* problem was getting that darn recipe book.

"Do any of you know of someone named Daisy that Adelaide would've been friendly with?" I asked.

The four of them exchanged blank looks and shrugs. They shook their heads.

"Daisy? I don't think we had a Daisy," Bing said.

"We've all got all kinds of other flowers though. There's Lily Mae Whitaker and then Rose Claremont and Ivy Schute." Cordelia ticked the names off on her fingers.

"Ivy isn't a flower, it's a vine," Hattie pointed out.

"Well, anyway, there's no Daisy. If there were, Josiah would know about it, wouldn't you?" Cordelia looked at Josiah, who nodded his head. Josiah was the former postmaster in town. He knew everything about everyone and where they lived. He also kept abreast of town happenings by still hanging around the post office during the day even though he'd retired almost twenty years ago.

"Why do you ask?" Bing appraised me thoughtfully with sparkling blue eyes.

"Oh, no reason. I just thought Gram mentioned someone named Daisy, and I didn't see her at the services yesterday." Another lie. This one was easier. Maybe I was getting better at it.

Bing pressed his lips together. "No. I don't remember any Daisy, but maybe Adelaide had friends I didn't know about. I wasn't that close to her. What about you, Hattie and Cordelia?"

"Not really. I mean, we were in the ladies' auxiliary together back in the fifties, and there was the fondue club in the seventies, but we hadn't seen a lot of her lately," Hattie said.

"Now I guess we won't be seeing her at all." Cordelia's voice softened sadly.

"Hopefully her death wasn't too sudden and she had her affairs in order and said everything she'd wanted to say to her loved ones," Bing said.

Josiah snorted. "Well, at her age I should hope she would. Speaking of which, I better get back to the post office. We're discussing the rules of the annual checkers tournament, and I want to make sure I have my say."

He got up to leave, and the others drained their cups. Disappointment washed over me. I had hoped I could find this Daisy person, retrieve the recipe book, and be done with Adelaide by dinnertime. But no one had heard of a Daisy, and between the four of them, my regulars knew everyone in town. I might've misheard Adelaide, though. Her voice had been fading out, her words garbled. Maybe she'd said something else, but what? Dusty? Lazy? Hazy? I'd either have to wait until she reappeared to get more specifics or hope something clicked into place during my search for the book.

"Come on, sister, I want to go by the cemetery and put some flowers on Adelaide's grave." Hattie tugged Cordelia off the couch.

"Good idea. I doubt her awful family will leave flowers." Cordelia stopped at the door and looked back at me. "You'll let us know if Gus mentions anything about Adelaide's passing, won't you?" She glanced behind her to make sure no new customers were around and then cupped her hand over her mouth as she stage whispered, "My money is on one of her relatives."

"Now, sister, come on. She likely died of natural causes." Hattie pulled Cordelia out the door. The last one to leave was Bing, who winked at me as he closed the door behind him.

Cordelia's parting words made me nervous. Adelaide had implied someone in her family might have had something to do with her demise. Maybe it couldn't hurt to find out what Gus knew about her death. Adelaide hadn't asked me to find her killer, and I had no intention of investigating her death, but it might be in my best interest to find out if there was foul play. If someone in her family was up to no good, it would be good to know so I could watch my back while I was looking for the recipe book.

"*Meow.*" Pandora had trotted over to me. She hopped up on the table and snaked her paw out to bat at my cell phone.

"Good idea. I can just call Gus and find out what she thinks."

I picked up the phone and punched in Gus's number.

"Hi, Willa. What's going on?" Gus asked.

"Not much. Just haven't talked in a while, so I thought I'd give you a call. You doing okay?"

Gus and I weren't particularly close as sisters go. I'd left Mystic Notch to go to college, and she'd stayed, going to law school nearby and eventually becoming the sheriff. I'd only returned a few years ago, but since I'd lived five hours away, we had never had a lot of face time together. We'd gotten together for various holidays with our parents and Gram and talked on the phone, but the truth was that the two of us really didn't know each other that well. Now that I was a permanent resident in the notch, that was all changing. We were becoming closer. We even shared a few secrets like the one where Gus played piano at a jazz bar in her off time. But we still didn't gab on the phone every day.

"I'm great. How about you? How was your date with Striker last night?" she asked.

Jeepers, did the whole town know when we had a date? "How did you know we had a date? Are you spying on me?"

Gus laughed. "Hardly. Jimmy saw him down at the Silver Maple picking up Chinese food, and he reported back to me."

"Oh." Jimmy was one of Gus's deputies. In Mystic Notch everyone knew everyone else's business. I guess I shouldn't expect to be any different. I didn't like talking about my and Striker's personal life, though, so I changed the subject. "I didn't see you at Adelaide Hamilton's wake yesterday."

Gus paused. "Should I have gone?"

"She was a friend of Gram's. Besides, someone dies in this town, you'd think it would be your business."

"Are you trying to tell me you think she was murdered?"

"Could she have been?"

"She died peacefully in her sleep. Not every death in this town is a murder, Willa."

Gus's voice had a guarded tone. Since I'd come back to the notch, I'd had to get involved in a few murder investigations. I didn't really want to, but the ghosts pestered me, and in order to get rid of them I had to do what the police weren't doing. Gus hated it when I "meddled." But her tone also told me that she had no reason to suspect Adelaide's death and no intention of opening an investigation.

Adelaide was an old woman with cancer. It surely wasn't out of the realm of possibility that she would die, even if the cancer was in remission. And just because Adelaide hinted that someone had murdered her ... well, that didn't mean it was true.

I dropped the subject, and Gus and I made small talk for a few more minutes then disconnected. Of course Gus was right about Adelaide dying from natural causes. Cordelia was the same age as Adelaide, so it made sense she would see Adelaide as being too young to die. She was an old woman, and she was sick. No one murdered her. At least I hoped not, because otherwise my trip to the Hamilton estate to look for Betty's recipes at noontime was going to be a lot more dangerous than I'd anticipated.

Chapter 7

The Hamilton mansion sat on several acres of fields, woods, and landscaped yard. The main house was three stories faced in limestone and of a classically elegant design. It sat at the end of a sweeping driveway lined with colorful flower beds and lush budding shrubs.

It was an older house, built in the early 1900s, and the estate included several additional buildings. One was a large barn and another I assumed a servants' or gardener's quarters. I parked my Jeep in front of the house, pushed away a flurry of nerves, and knocked on the oversized wooden door.

The knock received almost immediate attention, the door opening to reveal an actual butler. I was speechless for a moment, as I didn't realize people even still had butlers. He looked down at me, his lips pursed and his left brow raised. "Yes?"

"I'm Willa Chance. I'd like to pay my respects to the Hamiltons. My grandmother was a close friend of Adelaide."

"Certainly." He opened the door to let me in, his nose wrinkling as if I were a vagrant come to beg for dinner. "They're in the drawing room."

The house was lavishly furnished. Expensive antiques. Rich mahogany walls. Black-and-white marble floor. Stained glass. It smelled of lemon Pledge and old money. Tasteful arrangements of fresh flowers colored the room, and I wondered if they were from Adelaide's service or part of the usual household decor.

My sneakers made squeaky sounds on the marble as I followed the butler down the hall. Voices drifted from a room at the end of the hallway.

"...will...you have no..." A mature woman's voice. Josie or Lisa?

"No fair...of us..."

"...no arguing..." This was a man, probably the son, David.

"...sure I get my due—" Lisa bit off the end of the sentence, noticing the butler and me in the doorway. Her face creased in an angry frown as she looked me up and down in obvious disapproval. Should I have dressed up? I'd worn sneakers, jeans, and a T-shirt. The Hamiltons, who were all now staring at me, weren't dressed any more formally, except their T-shirts and jeans had fancy designer labels.

"Ms. Willa Chance." The butler announced me then disappeared into the woodwork, leaving me alone in the doorway.

"Hi." I plastered on a smile, extending my hand toward David and marching into the room. "My grandmother, Anna Chance, was good friends with Adelaide. I just wanted to pay my respects. I didn't have a chance to talk to any of you at the services yesterday."

As I shook David's limp, sweaty hand, my eyes strayed around the room, looking for errant recipe books that might be lying around.

"I'm her son, David. This is my wife, Lisa, and my sister, Josie." He gestured to the two women.

I shook hands with them, only half paying attention to them as I scoped out the room for the book. To my disappointment, there was not one bookcase in sight. The furniture was a mix of modern and Victorian. Comfortable and stuffy. High-backed chairs with light-blue velvet upholstery and carved mahogany trim kept company with a comfortable-looking sofa in off-white linen. Embroidered pillows matching the light blue of the chairs were scattered on the sofa. A glass-and-mahogany coffee table sat in front of it, a box of tissues stationed in the middle. Underfoot, a navy-blue-and-gold Oriental rug set atop oak flooring anchored the room. The rug was large enough to reach almost to the walls, which were done in what looked like a pale-blue satin wallpaper.

David shuffled his feet as we murmured greetings, then said, "Well, thanks for stopping by. I really have to get going. I'll leave you ladies to it."

We watched him disappear, then I turned to Lisa and Josie. "I'm so sorry about your loss, really. It must have been a shock."

Josie stared at me, glassy eyed. She opened her mouth but then snapped it shut.

"Yes, I suppose it was," Lisa said matter-of-factly. "She went to bed that night and never woke up."

"Oh, so one of you found her?" I asked.

Lisa smirked. "Not me. Marion did, I think."

"Yes, it's always hard, even when someone is sick and the death is expected." I leaned back to glance out the doorway into the hall. Had I seen a kitchen at the end of the hall? Is that where Adelaide would keep her recipe books? How could I get into it? Why couldn't Adelaide spring up now and give me some direction?

"Yes, it is. But Mom had a good long life," Josie said.

"I know. My grandma mentioned her often. They used to do a lot of baking together, I think. Did Adelaide still bake?" I asked casually.

"What?" Josie looked at me funny.

Lisa studied her crimson nails. "No. We have a cook for that."

"Oh, that's too bad. Gram said she had some special recipes. I bet she used to make them when you were young." I directed my words at Josie.

"Recipes?" Josie's eyes misted. "Now that you mention it, I do remember my mom used to bake cookies when I was younger."

"Gram said they shared recipe books with their friend Betty ... If you knew where that book is, I'd be really interested in seeing it—"

Squeaky wheels interrupted our conversation, and I turned to see Marion rolling into the room.

"Interested in what?" Marion demanded, her wrinkled face appraising me sharply.

Lisa waved a hand in the air. "Some recipe book her grandmother and some lady named Betty had. Who knows where that would be now."

"Your grandmother?" Marion scowled at me.

"Yes. Anna Chance," I said.

"Oh right ... yes. You have her hair." Marion chuckled then muttered something under her breath that sounded like "poor thing." "Who is Betty?"

"I don't know. I guess Adelaide knew her..."

Marion's brows dipped. "Betty? No. Do you know a Betty, Josie?"

"No."

"There's no Betty that I know of." Marion wheeled her chair around to face me. I noticed she was pretty good with it, easily avoiding smacking into the furniture. "You say you came for some recipes? Adelaide used to make a mean mince pie. I can get Cook to write out the recipe if you want. We don't have any old recipe books. Cook uses that confounded Internet."

"Oh, that won't be necessary." I tried to hide my disappointment. It didn't sound as if Betty's recipe book would be in the kitchen, but that wasn't the only place a person could hide a book in this mansion. If only I could figure out how to search the rest of the house.

"Well, it was nice of you to come by, then." Marion cast a glance at the door, and I got the hint.

I rose to leave. "If I can do anything for you ..."

"We'll get along just fine on our own. Always have," Marion said.

I wanted to ask about Daisy, but Marion's presence seemed to have shut down any talking on the part of Lisa and Josie, and by the way Marion had just dismissed me, I didn't want to push my luck. Not only that, but I was hoping to exit the room before someone offered to escort me out so I could take a quick look around the rest of the house. I could pretend I got lost looking for the bathroom if anyone questioned me.

Josie made a halfhearted attempt to get out of her chair, but I waved her off. "I can find my own way out." To my relief, she sank back down. I nodded to Lisa and Marion then scooted out into the hall.

As I tiptoed away from the room, I could hear Marion's voice. "Well, are you girls going to sit in here and do nothing all day? I suppose you're already spending your inheritance ..."

Instead of taking a right toward the front door, I turned left toward where I thought the kitchen was. Even though Marion said there were no recipe books, I wanted to peek in there for myself. But before I got more than a few steps down the hall, I heard something behind me.

Evie and Julie were coming down the stairs just as someone knocked on the front door. Julie skipped down the last three steps, pulling the door open to reveal a tall, good-looking man about the same age as the girls. I remembered him from Adelaide's service. He'd been hanging close to Julie. By the way he was looking at her, it appeared he was her boyfriend.

"Brian!" Julie gushed. From my vantage point, I could see the side of her face, the smile rounding her flushed cheekbones as she reached out and pulled Brian inside. Evie's face, on the other hand, darkened at the sight of her sister's boyfriend. Her brows slashed together. Clearly she did not like the young man. I couldn't say I blamed her. He gave me the impression of one of those charmers that had ulterior motives underneath. Probably after the Hamilton money, though Julie was quite attractive and seemed like a nice girl.

Evie started to turn in my direction, and my instincts kicked in. If she saw me, I'd surely have to leave. I quickly ducked into the nearest room, flattened myself against the wall, and held my breath.

"Did you see someone down there?" Evie's voice drifted down the hall.

"What?" This was from Julie. "No one is down there. Let's go walk the gardens."

Their voices faded away. I released my breath and looked around. The room was dark and filled with bookcases on three walls. A library! A shaft of sunlight spilled through thin windows on the far wall, highlighting tiny specks of dust that hung suspended in the air. The air carried that old, papery scent of vanilla and mildew. The silence was heavy, the volumes of reading material acting like insulation soaking up any of the noises beyond the room.

I could tell the room wasn't often used. The books sat patiently on the shelves as if waiting for someone to read them. A pair of wingback chairs were angled next to each other in front of a low oak table. On the other side of the table, a long tufted-back sofa in a green velvet upholstery begged for a reader to curl up on its worn cushions. There was a reading nook in one corner of the room. Inset into the wall, it provided a secluded place to escape into a book, complete with a burgundy velvet drape covering the opening and a comfortable-looking U-shaped cushioned seat with plump pillows. The sections of wall that weren't covered with bookshelves boasted rich brown mahogany panels, each with an ornate gilt-framed painting. They were some of the ugliest paintings I'd ever seen, including one of an early-twentieth-century gentleman surrounded by poodles and another of a lady in a long white gown standing in a field of white flowers—a daisy patch.

Maybe Adelaide had been talking about daisy flowers, not a person named Daisy.

I rushed over to the painting. The yellow-centered flowers with white petals were definitely daisies. Maybe the book was nearby. I ran my finger over the spines of the books that lined the shelves underneath the painting. Dust puffed up and floated in the air. The leather on the spines was dark with age, but the titles stamped in gold could easily be read. Poetry books. Old novels. But no recipe books.

"What are you doing snooping around in here?" I whirled around to see Marion had snuck up behind me. I'd been so intent on looking for the recipe book that I hadn't heard her wheels squeaking.

"Sorry. I was looking for the bathroom ..."

"There's no bathroom in here. I thought you were leaving."

The butler appeared in the doorway, and Marion swung the chair around to face him. "John. Our guest can't seem to find the front door. Can you show her out?"

"Of course." John stepped aside in an obvious gesture for me to proceed out into the hall. I reluctantly left my spot under the picture. As I stepped out into the hall, I glanced back at the books under the picture just in case I suddenly spotted the recipe book. But it wasn't a book that caught my eye. It was something outside the window next to the bookcase. The window gave a picturesque view of the grounds behind the mansion. In the distance I could see a quaint stone cottage—servants' quarters, I guessed. But that wasn't what interested me the most. The cottage was sitting smack-dab in the middle of a field of daisies.

My heart skittered with excitement as I continued down the hall, John following one step behind me the entire way as if to make sure I actually left this time. He opened the door for me, and I got the feeling he wanted to push me through it but was too polite to actually do so. I stepped outside, and he promptly shut the door.

As I walked to my car, I craned my neck to try to see behind the house. It was too big, though. I couldn't see the field. But now I knew it was back there. Too bad I had no idea how to actually get to it. A stone path meandered around the side of the house through the gardens. Was that the only access, or was there a road that connected to the cottage from the other side?

I doubted Adelaide had buried the recipe book in a field. If she had, it would be ruined by now, but maybe she'd hidden it in the stone house. There was only one way to find out. I had to get to that field and the house beyond it, but how could I possibly do that without raising the suspicions of the Hamiltons?

Chapter 8

Pandora sulked in the bookstore window. She hated it when Willa refused to include her in her outings. Even more than that, she didn't appreciate Willa's assumptions that Pandora might screw things up or run off. She should know by now that Pandora could take care of herself and knew how to conduct herself at someone else's house.

Looking around the bookstore, she wondered what she could do to express her displeasure. Maybe a hairball in the cookbook aisle? Or she could run the toilet paper off the roll in the bathroom. That was always fun, but she'd done it so many times now Willa didn't seem as shocked anymore when she came in and discovered a river of toilet paper throughout the store.

Maybe it was best if she didn't do anything. That would keep Willa on her toes. And it might earn her some brownie points. Maybe even get her a taste of Willa's tuna fish sandwich if she were to have one for lunch. Or possibly even some catnip.

Yes, doing nothing was probably the best course of action. Pandora stretched then repositioned herself in her cat bed so that the sun was warming her back.

Purring contentedly, her eyes were just slitting closed when she saw Him.

He was trotting down the sidewalk beside his human. Two evil beings looking as if they hadn't a care in the world. The worst thing about them was that from all outside appearances they seemed perfectly innocent. The human, Felicity Bates, looked normal enough with her pale skin and red hair. The fluffy white Persian cat trotting beside her looked cute. Cuddly even. His name was Fluff, and he was anything but cute and cuddly.

The hair on Pandora's back stood on end as she watched them move closer to the bookstore. Pandora had had a run-in with Fluff not that long ago, and it had nearly killed her. She'd had to go up against him to keep the young chimera cat, Hope, from falling into the clutches of the dark side, of which Fluff was a member. Though Mystic Notch was indeed a special town with a heightened sense of magic, it was no different than any other place where, according to the laws of nature, there must be balance. Just as Pandora and the cats in Elspeth's barn were sworn to keep Mystic Notch on the side of "good," there were other cats, especially Fluff, who wanted the notch to swing to the side of "evil."

Pandora stared out the window at Fluff's malevolent amber eyes. She arched her back and hissed. Fluff's whiskers twitched in amusement.

"Your side is in a little trouble," he hissed.

"I've no idea what you mean." Pandora tried to act nonchalant. What did he mean?

"You seek a book, do you not?" He stared at her unblinkingly.

Pandora tried not to react, but he must have sensed her surprise. His tail flicked, and he moved closer to the window, his human obliviously gazing across the street, probably trying to decide whether to go into the hat store or the new photography shop.

"I happen to know that one of the Hamilton clan covets the book you seek. They are very close to possessing it, and you will not get it for your purposes." Fluff smirked.

"How do you know that?" Pandora doubted that Fluff knew anything. He was a liar and was probably just trying to get her all riled up. But if that were the case, how did he even know about the Hamiltons' connection to the book in the first place?

"My human knows the Hamiltons quite well ... at least some of them. They are of the same mind." Fluff glanced up at Felicity, who turned to face them. Her ruby lips curled in a smile, she bent down and petted Fluff behind the ears.

"That may be, but my human can beat the pants off your human any day. We'll get the book," Pandora said childishly.

Felicity straightened and glared into the window at her as if she could understand cat-speak. Pandora doubted she could. Felicity wasn't the sharpest pencil in the box.

"Come on now. You can talk to your little friend later." Felicity waggled a shiny red talon at Pandora as she tugged Fluff away.

Fluff glanced over his shoulder and delivered a parting shot. "I doubt that. We'll see who gets the book. You, your human, and your gang of cats are no match for my human. Why, I have her so well trained now, I don't have to do any of the dirty work myself."

Pandora's stomach tightened as she watched them sashay down the street. Her whiskers twitched uneasily.

Darn it! Fluff knew something about the book, though how much he knew wasn't clear. What had he meant about one of the Hamiltons being of like mind? Was one of Adelaide's relatives af-

ter that book? If so, that could be very bad for her and Willa. A relative would have much easier access to Adelaide's hiding spot. But Willa had access to Adelaide. Maybe the ghost would show up and reveal the location of the book. Pandora didn't dare hope for that. Things were never that easy.

Pandora settled back into her cat bed with a heavy sigh. She'd hoped that the dual ghosts of Louis and Adelaide spurring both Willa and Striker on to find the book would have brought the matter to a quick close and left Pandora with little to do but nap and feast. But now Fluff had issued a challenge, and Pandora was not one to back down from a challenge. Not to mention that if Fluff had spoken the truth about a villain from the Hamilton clan trying to secure the book, then that made the search much more urgent.

From what Pandora could tell, Willa wasn't putting a high priority on finding the book, though she had gone to the Hamiltons' today in search of it. Maybe they would luck out and she would come back with it, but if she didn't, Pandora would have to do something to prod her human into quick action.

It was time to dial her cat-to-human telepathy skills up to the next level. She just prayed that Willa would finally become a ready receiver.

Chapter 9

When I returned to the bookstore, I was surprised to find that Pandora hadn't done anything to exact her revenge for being left alone. Or at least not anything that I could find. Her behavior made me suspicious, though. She was acting sweet, rubbing up against me and looking at me at me innocently with those golden-green eyes.

Too sweet and too innocent. It set me on edge —the behavior was out of character for the normally feisty and contrarian feline. Maybe she'd done something that I had yet to discover.

I didn't have much time to look for it, though. The bookstore was crowded with customers most of the afternoon, and I was kept busy ringing in sales. Adelaide's ghost was nowhere to be seen, not that I would've had time to talk to her. But I'd hoped she would show up when I closed the shop and give me some kind of direction for the search. No such luck. There wasn't a swirl of mist or hint of ectoplasmic dew. Not even Robert or Franklin appeared to chat. Must have been something interesting going on over on the other side.

"Maybe Adelaide's gone on and I won't have to find that stupid book to get her to stop haunting me after all," I said to Pandora later that night at home as I kicked back on my couch, my feet propped up on the coffee table.

"*Mewooo!*" Pandora leapt up on the coffee table and batted at the crystal paperweight that Elspeth had given to me as a housewarming gift when I'd moved in.

"Don't smash that on the floor." I leaned forward and moved the paperweight away from her into the center of the table. As I moved it, the crystal orb flashed, reflecting a rainbow of light. For a second, though, I thought I saw a field of daisies inside. I leaned closer, squinting into the orb. Not daisies, just a weird reflection from the ceiling.

"Cripes, now I'm seeing daisies everywhere," I muttered to myself.

"*Menow.*" Pandora gave up on the paperweight and crawled into my lap. She'd been clingy and cuddly all day, which was a nice switch from her normal aloof and independent personality. I rubbed her silky gray fur, soothed by the low vibration of her purr. She gazed at me with unblinking luminescent eyes. I felt a strange vibe. Almost like a connection, but then I felt a pang of alarm. Something wasn't right with Pandora. She'd been staring at me in that strange manner ever since I got back from the Hamiltons'. I hoped there wasn't something wrong with her. She wasn't due for her checkup for another three months, but maybe I should take her in early just to be sure.

"*Meowoo.*"

"What? You don't want to go to the vet?" It was almost as if she knew what I was thinking.

"*Meaisy.*"

"Yes, I need to check out that field of daisies. And the cottage," I said absently.

"*Meow.*"

"Not now. It's dark out, and besides, that daisy field was behind the mansion. I can't just go marching through the Hamiltons' yard to get there."

I guess Pandora didn't have an answer to that one, because she simply kept staring up at me.

A strange dream-like feeling came over me, and old memories drifted up from somewhere deep in my subconscious. As a teenager, I'd joy-ridden on all the roads in the notch extensively. Especially the out-of-the-way back roads. And if I was remembering correctly, there was a dirt road not far from the Hamiltons' driveway. Maybe that road led to the stone cottage?

"*Meow!*"

Pandora sprang off my lap and trotted toward the kitchen door as if encouraging me to investigate whether or not my teenage memories were true. What the heck? It was dark out, and I had nothing better to do and nothing to lose. I could just drive out and see if there was a road that led to the cottage. Maybe take a little peek in the windows? I was sure it was empty. What harm could it do?

Happy to have a plan of action, I sprang up off the couch and followed Pandora. I grabbed my hoodie from the pegs next to the door. Even though it was warm enough out, it would protect me from mosquitoes, and the hood over my face would help me blend in with the shadows.

Pandora was already halfway out her cat door. She looked back at me and gave an impatient meow. As usual, she wanted to come with me, and I could tell from her stubborn stance that she wasn't going to take no for an answer.

"Okay, this time you can come with me, but you better behave." She shot through the cat door and across the driveway toward my Jeep before I even had a chance to get out the door.

***

I found the road about a quarter of a mile past the mansion. It was a narrow dirt road that one could easily miss. Judging by the grass growing in between the tire ruts, not many drove down it. I turned off my headlights so no one would see them from the mansion and let the parking lights illuminate the way as I drove slowly down the road. Pandora thumped her tail against the passenger seat in excited anticipation.

The cottage was about an eighth of a mile down the road. The silver half-moon provided enough light to see it fairly clearly but still offered good cover. Across the field, amber lights blazed in the mansion, but it was too far away for anyone to see me. A green pinpoint glow could be seen in one of the cottage windows. Probably an appliance or maybe even an alarm system. If the cottage was empty, and it made sense, they would have an alarm with it being so far from the house. I'd have to be careful not to set it off if I looked in the windows.

I parked a couple hundred feet down from the cottage on the opposite side of the road, hopped over the stone wall, and picked my way through the tall grass to the field. I breathed in the subtle, sweet smells of honeysuckle and hay as Pandora trotted at my side, expertly snaking her way through the grass.

I wasn't really sure what I was looking for. Some help would be nice.

"Adelaide? I could use some help now," I whispered, hoping to conjure the ghost, but all I heard were the chirping of crickets and leaves rustling in the light breeze.

"*Mew.*" Pandora gave me a look.

"I know. They never show up when you want them to," I whispered.

"*Meow.*"

With Pepper on vacation and Gus and Striker occupied with police business, I hadn't had a lot of people to talk to this week. But even though I was a natural loner, I was starting to get afraid that I might've been spending too much time alone, because I was starting to imagine that Pandora could understand me. Not only that, but it almost seemed as if we had some sort of a communication channel going.

Nah, that was silly, I thought. But something niggled in the back of my brain. I'd known for a long time that Pandora wasn't like ordinary cats. She seemed to be smarter, more intuitive. I knew for a fact that she'd been special to Gram. Was there really a connection between us? It seemed far-fetched, but considering I'd just tried to conjure a ghost, maybe communicating with my cat wasn't so out of the ordinary. Perhaps I should pay more attention to Pandora when it appeared as if she was trying to tell me something.

"*Meow!*"

We stood at the edge of the daisy field. It was a pretty big field, much bigger than it looked from the mansion. The moon reflected off the white petals, turning them a silver-blue. A flagstone path cut down the middle of the daisies and curved toward the stone cottage. I realized I had no idea where to start looking.

Adelaide had said the word "daisies," but she couldn't have meant she buried the book, could she? A book would be ruined pretty quickly if it were buried in the damp earth. What if she'd put it inside something to protect it? Tupperware or some kind of box, maybe. Why would she go to such great lengths?

Unlike me, Pandora wasn't one to stand around and ponder. She trotted to a spot in the middle of the field and started digging.

"What are you doing?" I whispered.

She stopped, looked back at me as if I had just asked the stupidest question ever, and then turned back to her digging. I walked over beside her, taking out my cell phone and using the flashlight app to illuminate the ground in front of her. I didn't have cat eyes that could see in the dark as she could.

She'd torn out some of the flowers and had dug down about an inch into the earth. I trained the beam around the area. Flowers were squished and flattened. Someone had been here recently, but the damage didn't look like footprints. It was more like narrow tracks.

I squatted to inspect the ground further. It did look as if someone had been digging, but they'd also carefully replaced the flowers and topsoil.

"What's going on over here?"

I dropped the phone, my heart crashing against my rib cage as I whirled around to see a dark, ominous figure standing at the edge of the field.

Chapter 10

The ominous figure was Striker. His arms were crossed over his chest, and his steely gaze flicked from my face to Pandora's. On the one hand, I was relieved it was him and not some creepy weirdo. On the other, I might rather face a creepy weirdo than have to try to explain why I was out here in the middle of the night.

"So what is it? Why are you here?" he demanded.

I squatted down to retrieve my phone and give myself time to make up an excuse. But what kind of excuse could one have for being out in the middle of a field in the middle of the night?

"I was just looking for Pandora," I said lamely.

Pandora meowed loudly as if to lend credence to my lie.

The cottage door whipped open, and a figure appeared in the doorway. It was Adelaide's grandson Max, and he looked angry.

"What the hell are you doing on our property?" He stormed over to where Pandora had been digging. "Were you digging up my time capsule?"

"Time capsule?" Striker and I said at the same time. What was he talking about? Was Adelaide's recipe book in some kind of time capsule?

"I'm calling the police," Max said.

Striker flashed his badge. "I am the police. I'll escort Ms. Chance from the premises."

"Miss Chance?" Max squinted at me. "Aren't you that lady who inherited the bookstore from my grandma's friend?"

"Yes, that's me."

That seemed to make him less adversarial, and Striker took the opportunity to grab my elbow and pull me away.

"I'll see that she doesn't bother you anymore," he shot over his shoulder as he dragged me back toward the road.

"Hey, what about Pandora?" I looked around for the cat, but she was nowhere to be found.

"She can take care of herself," Striker said. "You're lucky I showed up when I did. Who knows what that guy would have done."

I pulled my arm away and narrowed my eyes at him. "And exactly why *did* you show up there?"

Striker's face hardened, and I noticed he couldn't look me in the eye. Instead he turned toward his car. "Never mind why *I* was there. Why were *you* there? I could put you in jail for trespassing."

It didn't escape me that he had evaded my question. Which made me wonder if there really was something to Adelaide's accusations that someone in her family had killed her. If not, why would Striker be out at the Hamilton estate investigating? A seed of uneasiness sprouted in my stomach. If one of Adelaide's relatives was a killer, it could make nosing around for the recipe book a lot more dangerous than I had anticipated.

"So you were looking for the murder weapon in that time capsule," I persisted.

"Murder weapon?" He did a good impersonation of someone being surprised, but that didn't fool me. "What are you talking about?"

"You guys must think Adelaide was murdered. That's why you're here, isn't it?"

"No...I mean it's none of your business why I'm here, but I wasn't looking for any murder weapon in a time capsule."

"Of course, there wouldn't really be a weapon," I realized. "If she'd been stabbed, bludgeoned, or shot, no one would think she died of natural causes. It must've been something more subtle like poison or suffocation." But then why would Striker be in this field in the middle of the night?

"You think everything has to do with murder. But you're wrong in this case. There is no evidence to indicate Adelaide was murdered, so I have no probable cause to investigate it. I just happened to be on patrol, and I saw your Jeep here. I know how you like to stick your nose in where it doesn't belong, and I was worried that you might be in trouble, so I came to see if you needed my help, Chance."

Had he really been worried about me? My heart melted at the way his voice softened when he said my last name. It was a pet name he used for me. According to Striker, my last name was appropriate because I took a lot of chances.

We stopped beside Striker's police car. I looked around for Pandora. She'd disappeared when Max had come out of his cottage, and I was a little worried about her.

"She'll be fine. I saw her trot up the road ahead of us." Striker was standing very close, and I backed up a step, my butt meeting the side of the car's passenger door. He leaned one palm against the roof, trapping me. He brushed a lock of hair behind my ear with his other hand. "So what gives? Why were you out here? And I'm not buying that story about looking for Pandora."

I sure as heck couldn't tell him I was out there because a ghost had sent me looking for a recipe book, so I decided to ignore his question. "Are you going to arrest me for trespassing?"

Striker leaned even closer, kicking my pulse up a notch. "If I ever get you in handcuffs, I promise a jail cell won't be involved."

I didn't have a good comeback for that, especially since I was distracted by the way his lips were hovering close to mine. I leaned toward him, and he brushed his lips against mine then, much to my disappointment, pulled back and planted a chaste kiss on my forehead.

"I'm going to just let you off with a warning this time. Come on, I'll drive you back to your car." He opened the door for me, and I slipped in.

He started up the car and drove the short distance to my Jeep. I was relieved to see Pandora sitting on the hood, leisurely cleaning her face. Striker put the car in park and then swiveled to face me, his arm up on top of the seat.

"Look. I know you like to keep your journalistic skills honed by looking into these murders, but I think you're barking up the wrong alley with Adelaide. She was an old woman who died in her sleep."

"I know. I wasn't actually looking into any murder ..."

Striker looked skeptical. His warm hand clasped over mine, and he brought it to his lips then brushed a kiss over my knuckles that sent butterflies swarming in my stomach. "You have a talent for getting into danger. If there wasn't already a murder, I get the feeling you would incite one. I don't want anything to happen to you ... so I hope you'll be careful."

At least he hadn't asked me to stay away from the Hamiltons. He was distracting me with the kissing. Another minute, and I might agree to backing off entirely. I pulled my hand back gently, opened the door and stepped out, then leaned back in and blew him a kiss. "I promise I'll be careful."

"I'm going to hold you to that. And I hope you are going straight home," he said out his car window as Pandora and I hopped into my Jeep.

"I am." I did a three-point turn and headed for the main road, waving to him in the rearview mirror as I turned toward town.

Striker followed me back to town. I had to admit I was a little disappointed when his car turned off instead of going all the way to my house, but then again he had said he was on duty. If that were the case, what was he doing out patrolling near the Hamilton estate? I was sure the police didn't patrol that far out.

Striker had said he'd seen my car and thought I might be in trouble, but my Jeep had been parked too far down the dirt road to be seen from the main road. The only way he could have seen it was if he had also been driving down the dirt road. Which made me wonder just exactly what Eddie Striker was up to.

Chapter 11

Pandora wasn't sure the daisy field was the right place to look for the book. She knew something was buried there, but she hadn't sensed a magical aura. She knew that the earth dampened any magic buried beneath it. Still, she felt deep down in her gut that the book was not buried. Hidden, but not buried. Her twitching whiskers told her they had been close, though, when they'd been interrupted by Striker.

Her tail swished on the wide pine floorboards of Willa's bedroom as she watched the human get ready for bed. She had to admit, she was a little disappointed they'd had to call the search off early, but it was late at night, and she knew humans needed their rest. They didn't have all day to lounge around napping, as cats did.

Luckily their foray to the Hamilton cottage had not been in vain. She had learned something important. She'd seen no evidence of the evil Fluff. Not a whisper of his scent or a strand of white cat hair to indicate he had been in the area. Which meant that he was not yet onto the same trail. How long that would last she didn't know, but at least for now they had a head start.

It did appear, though, as if Striker was onto the same trail. This was a good sign, as Pandora knew Striker was also looking for the recipe book on instructions from Louis's ghost. But what clues did Striker have that they didn't?

There was only one way to find out.

Pandora waited for Willa to get settled into bed before slipping out of the room to the kitchen and silently exiting through the cat door.

The night was still. The moon and stars glowed in the cloudless sky, but Pandora didn't need them to light the way. She had near-perfect night vision normally and even better vision when she kicked her superior senses into high gear, which she was now doing so as to heighten her sense of smell in order to locate Striker.

She stuck to the edges of the forest, not going in too deep. Though she was ferocious in battle, there was no sense tempting fate. The woods were full of bobcats and coyotes as well as other creatures that might see her as a tasty meal. When she traveled with the other Mystic Notch cats, she never worried about predators—there was safety in numbers. But tonight she would travel alone. It took time to summon the others, and she needed to find Striker before he, too, retired for the night.

She raced toward town, her nose sniffing the air in an attempt to catch his scent. She sped past the lingering aromas of family dinners, the sharp fear of a small child having a nightmare, the contentment of an old dog snuggling into the warm blankets at the foot of his owner's bed, and finally just a whiff of the spicy scent that was Striker.

His scent led her down a side street that led to the First Hope Church. It being the middle of the night, naturally the church was closed. The parking lot was empty except for Striker's police car. Striker leaned against the hood, his hands gesturing wildly. At first it looked strange because Striker appeared to be alone, but as Pandora got closer she noticed the telltale misty swirl of a ghost. Louis Hamilton's ghost.

She stuck to the tree line, not wanting Striker or the ghost to see her. They were obviously in an animated conversation, and she didn't want to interrupt them, but she needed to get close enough to listen in. Crouching behind a thick scotch pine, she swiveled her ears like radar dishes and homed in on their voices.

Behind her, a barely visible path led to a secluded shelter deep in the woods. Pandora knew this shelter was for the many feral cats of Mystic Notch. Her heart swelled with pride as she thought of how often Willa took time out from her day to bring food, blankets, and water to these cats.

Pandora didn't know most of the cats well—many were wild and not magical like Elspeth's cats—but she still felt a deep kinship with them and was happy they were cared for and sheltered. Tonight, however, that was not her concern. Her concern was finding out if Striker's conversation with Louis's ghost might yield an important clue that Pandora could use to nudge Willa in the right direction.

"What in tarnation is taking you so long to find that book?" Louis was saying. "It's not like I'm asking you to find a long-lost treasure. It's just one book, for crying out loud."

Striker ran his hand through his short-cropped hair, his agitation apparent to Pandora. "Well, if you would just tell me where it is, I'd be happy to oblige. You think I don't want to get rid of you? I'm looking over my shoulder all the time now, expecting to see you there. It's irritating."

"What are you talking about? I told you to go to the old gardener's cottage. Adelaide used to store stuff in there. Did you even look in there?"

"I can't look in there. Your grandson seems to be doing something in there now."

"Doing something in there? What?"

"I'm not sure, exactly."

"Hmm... probably something to do with his computers. I know Adelaide dotes on the boy. She probably gave him access to get him out of the house and away from his evil stepmother. He's quite brilliant, you know." Louis tapped his head. *"Gets his brains from me. Even though I died before he was born, I still got a right to be proud of him."*

"Then I don't know how I can look in there. I didn't get a chance to see anything when I was there because Willa was there. That really screwed things up for me because now she thinks I'm investigating a murder. Once she gets on the scent of a murder investigation, there's no pulling her off."

"Murder?" Louis swirled, concern creasing his ghostly features. *"Was my Adelaide murdered?"*

"No." Striker chewed his bottom lip. *"There's no evidence of that. Gus would've told me if there was."*

"Oh, good." Louis relaxed. *"But that's neither here nor there, I suppose. She's dead now either way. And I need that book to be able to get to her."*

"And you are absolutely certain that the book is in the cottage?"

"I can't say as I'm absolutely certain. It's one of the places Adelaide used to store stuff, but if

she's got Max in there now, she's likely moved her storage. Heck, I've been gone so long, for all I know someone in the family cleaned it out long ago. Like that money-grubbing Lisa. Do you know that the few times I've been able to manifest in the house I've caught her stealing the family silver? Literally!"

"Lisa?"

"Poor David. How he let that viper get her claws in him." Louis shook his head. "His first wife, Emily, was a sweet soul. She's gone through the golden gates now, lucky thing. She died when Max was just little, and I suppose David wanted someone to mother the poor boy. Too bad he didn't get what he expected."

Through the dark, Pandora could see Striker's steely eyes narrow on Louis, and she could sense his cop instincts kicking in. "What do you mean? You think Lisa could have taken this book? Why? Does she like cooking that much?"

"Maybe. Maybe she just wanted the book that Adelaide coveted. If Adelaide valued it, she might think it was worth something. I don't know, but I'll tell you one thing. If someone really did do something to my Adelaide, or the book, I wouldn't be surprised to find out it was her."

Chapter 12

The next morning I practically had to drag myself to the bookstore. I was tired from the previous night's foray into the daisy field. Pandora appeared even more tired than I was. She loped along slowly beside me and then snuggled into her cat bed in the window the moment we were inside.

The regulars weren't there yet, but I was greeted by Robert and Franklin, who drifted out from the History aisle to swirl beside the desk while I dumped my purse behind the counter and sorted through the sales receipts I'd left beside the cash register the day before.

"What's with you? You're as pale as a ghost." Robert snickered.

"Late night with Striker last night?" Franklin wiggled his white brows.

"No. Not really. Well, I did run into Striker, but I was out looking for that damn recipe book."

"Oh, still looking for that?" Franklin made a face then turned to Robert. "Did you find anything about recipes on the ghostly grapevine?"

"Not a thing, I'm afraid. Though my spiritual sources tell me there might be more at stake than just recipes," Robert said.

"Maybe they are recipes about steak." Franklin tittered.

"This isn't funny, guys. I have a feeling there might be more to this, too," I said.

"Oh?"

"I think Adelaide was murdered. Why else would Striker have been out at the Hamilton mansion last night?"

"*Meow!*" Pandora stirred in her bed, glaring at me from one slit eye.

"Right?" I agreed with her and then turned back to the ghosts. "See, even Pandora agrees."

"I do hope it's not going to be dangerous for you." Franklin swirled with concern, and warmth blossomed in my chest. He might just be a ghost, but it still made me feel good that he cared.

"Yes, Willa, you be careful." Robert glanced out the window, then his eyes widened. "We have to go, but you make sure to take care of yourself. You don't have to go miles before you sleep." He laughed at the reference to his own poem and then disappeared just as the door opened and Bing, Hattie, Cordelia, and Josiah came in.

" ... was getting her nails painted bright red and buying designer purses. Not even a decent time of mourning before she started spending the money," Cordelia was saying over her shoulder to Hattie as they made their way to the sofa.

"I just don't know what it is with young people these days. No respect." Hattie clucked.

Bing handed me a coffee in a Styrofoam cup as he walked past on his way to one of the chairs.

"Maybe you were right about Adelaide's death not being natural." Cordelia's words caught my attention, and I slipped out from behind the cash register to join them on the sofa.

"Why you do say that?" I asked.

Cordelia huffed, straightening the lapels of her sky-blue polyester jacket. Cordelia and Hattie, identical twins, often wore similar outfits. Today Cordelia had on a sky-blue pantsuit with a navy shirt, and Hattie had on a navy pantsuit with a sky-blue shirt. "Have you seen her around town? She's high in the instep, and she likes her creature comforts."

"It's true. Coloring her hair, getting her nails done, wearing the latest fashions. You know how it is." Hattie flicked her hand in the air.

"She thinks she's better than the rest of us. Or she wants to be, anyway," Cordelia said.

"It's all to draw the men's eyes, anyway," Hattie added.

"That's hardly a reason for her to kill Adelaide," Josiah pointed out.

I settled back on the sofa and sipped my coffee. The other day I had thought Hattie and Cordelia were just being fanciful with their suspicions concerning Adelaide's death. The ladies didn't have much to keep them amused, and their imaginations ran wild at times. But given what I'd learned over the past few days, I was starting to think there might be something to their theory.

On my visit to the Hamilton house, I'd overheard Lisa say something about being sure she got her "due." Had she been worried about her portion of Adelaide's will? But if she was uncertain about what she would inherit, why would she kill her? Why would anyone?

Striker had been skulking around the Hamilton mansion last night, *and* Adelaide had mentioned she thought someone in her family had killed her. Gus had denied any evidence of foul play, but maybe something new had come to light.

It didn't really matter, though. I wasn't on a mission to find Adelaide's killer. It might be true that she was murdered. And maybe Striker was investigating it, but Adelaide's ghost was only haunting me for the recipe book. This time I was going to keep my nose out of any ongoing murder investigation. Unless, of course, her killer had been after the recipe book all along. If that were the case, then figuring out who the killer was might help me find the book.

"You look tired, Willa. Is something bothering you?" Bing's eyes were full of concern, but I thought I caught a glimpse of something else. A knowing look, as if he could read my thoughts.

"Late night last night," I said noncommittally as I sipped my coffee.

Hattie raised her brows. "Oh? Out with that hunky young man of yours?"

My cheeks heated. "No. Well, not really." I fiddled with my cup. I wasn't about to tell them I'd been digging up the Hamilton estate in the middle of the night or that I'd run into Striker there.

As if thoughts of Striker conjured him, the door to the bookstore opened, and he stepped in with a white bag from the coffee shop down the street.

"We better be going, sister." Cordelia shot me a sly look, her eyes twinkling with excitement as she shot up off the sofa. She grabbed Hattie's hand, and the two of them greeted Striker as they brushed past him.

"I gotta get to the post office." Josiah stood and nodded a farewell to me then to Striker.

Bing had stood, too, and was making his way toward the door. "Looks like I better start the day, too. Unless you're here to arrest Willa," Bing joked with Striker as he clapped him on the shoulder on his way out the door.

"No. Not yet, at least." Striker watched them leave then held the bag out to me.

"What's this?" I peered into the bag, my mouth watering as I spied a glazed cruller and a Boston cream donut.

"A peace offering."

"Don't you have to work today?" I bit into the cruller, my taste buds doing a happy dance as the sugary glaze coated them.

"I do. But I wanted to make sure you were okay after last night."

"Why wouldn't I be?" Now my suspicions were on high alert. Bringing me donuts and stopping in to make sure I was okay? The circumstances surrounding Adelaide's death must be more nefarious than I'd thought.

Striker leaned against the counter. "No reason. I just didn't know if you went digging up anyone else's yard last night."

"Very funny." I finished the rest of the cruller. "So what's going on with Adelaide's death?"

Striker scowled. "Nothing."

"*Meow!*" Pandora had jumped down from her bed and was playing with one of her catnip toys. She batted it with her paw, and it slid across the floor, spinning to a stop in between Striker and me. I nudged it back across the room to her with my toe then looked back up at Striker.

"Nothing? Then why were you at the Hamiltons' last night?"

The toy came sliding back, catching Striker's attention, and he watched as Pandora slid over then used her left paw to bounce the toy off the side of his boot. "I told you I saw your car there."

"Nice try. My car was pretty far down the dirt road, so you must have been at the Hamilton estate in order to see it."

Pandora batted the toy again, and it skidded to a stop in between the toes of my blue-and-white-striped Keds. I frowned down at it, noticing exactly what the toy was—a white ghost. Was she trying to tell me something? She had been acting very perceptive lately. Maybe she knew something I didn't. I looked around nervously for Adelaide.

"I'm the police. I patrol the area." Striker glanced up from the toy, his eyes drifting around the room.

"But you're not the police in Mystic Notch." I was talking to Striker, but my eyes were still on alert for signs of Adelaide's ghost.

Pandora flipped the toy in the air and jumped up after it. She batted it in midair, and it flew across the room, landing at the end of the paranormal and mystical books aisle.

"Every place I go doesn't have to do with murder." Striker stepped closer to me and captured my wrist in his hand. "Honestly, I really just wanted to make sure you weren't getting into anything that you might not be able to get out of."

His thumb rubbed slow circles on the inside of my wrist, making me forget all about Pandora and her catnip toy. "Don't worry. I'm not looking into Adelaide's murder. I was there for another reason entirely."

Striker's brow creased. "What could you have possibly been there for—"

The bells over the door chimed, interrupting his question. A customer slipped in. From where I stood, I could only see him from the side. A young guy with a baseball cap pulled down over his face. He glanced at us quickly then darted behind Striker's back toward the aisle where I kept the comic books. Not unusual for a young person, but something about his demeanor set my nerves on edge.

Striker released my wrist and ran his hand through his short-cropped dark hair. "Okay, well, I've got to get back to work. You give me a call if you need me." He dropped a kiss on the top of my head and was gone.

I approached the comic aisle tentatively and nearly peed my pants when the customer peered out at me just as I peeked around the corner.

"Max?" I recognized Adelaide's grandson. Up close, I could see he was thin, with long brown bangs that fell in front of his eyes.

A sheepish look spread over his face, and he pushed the cap up higher on his head so I could see more of his face. "Sorry."

"Were you hiding from Striker?" I asked.

He scanned the store to make sure it was empty. "I need to tell you something, but the police can't know."

"Why tell me, then?" It seemed odd he wanted to confide in me today considering he wanted to kick me off his property just last night.

He leaned toward me, lowering his voice even though no one else was in the store. "I've done some checking on you. You're looking for Gram's killer, aren't you?"

"He always was such a good kid." Adelaide's ghost popped up out of nowhere, scaring the bejesus out of me. She swirled and glowed with pride. I ignored her and focused on Max.

"What makes you think someone killed her?"

"I don't know. A bad feeling, I guess." Max looked straight at Adelaide, but it was clear he couldn't see her. "I just sense it."

Adelaide snorted. "No wonder. I've been trying to alert him since the moment I died. He's smarter than he looks, I promise. And he has the gift like you—he's just not in tune with it yet. I don't think he's in any danger, but it doesn't hurt to be on one's toes."

"So what do you want to tell me?" I asked Max.

"You promise you won't tell the police? I mean, I'm not sure if she did anything…"

"I won't tell. Who aren't you sure about?"

"Aunt Josie wasn't there."

"She wasn't where?"

"In the house. On the property. The morning Gram was found. Everyone was yelling, and we called the ambulance, but Aunt Josie couldn't be found. I mean, even Julie's boyfriend was there with us." Max's brows drew together. "Though there was some speculation as to why he was in the house so early in the morning. Gram didn't like it when Julie snuck him into her room to… you know…"

Max's embarrassment over what Julie and Brian might have been doing in her room was cute, but I was more interested in Adelaide's body—if she'd been murdered, there might have been some signs that her death was not peaceful.

"Just exactly how was your grandmother found?"

Max shrugged. "She didn't get up for breakfast, I guess. Aunt Marion went in to get her up, and then she started screaming."

"And you're all usually in the house for breakfast?"

"Well, Dad, Lisa, and I live in the converted barn, but we usually go over in the morning. Cook puts out a big breakfast around seven-thirty. Josie, Marion, and the twins live in the house with Gram."

"So you think Josie killed her? Her own mother? Couldn't she have just died in her sleep?"

His eyes misted. "No. Not Gram. She was doing really good. The doctors even said so. We played Scrabble the night before, and she was happy ..."

"Did you see her?"

He nodded slightly and looked down at his sneakers. "She was just lying there like she was sleeping."

Darn. There would have been no sign of struggle or poison if she looked as if she'd died in her sleep ... unless someone had positioned her that way.

"But if Josie wasn't there, wouldn't that prove she *didn't* kill her?"

"Not if Gram died hours before. If she had something to do with it, she might have been out disposing of evidence." He pulled his phone out of his pocket. "My surveillance camera at the cottage captured her taking off in the car that morning."

He tilted the screen toward me, and I saw the Hamilton mansion in the distance. Josie appeared out a side door then scurried across the driveway to the five-stall garage. A few seconds later, the door opened, and out she drove in a shiny black Mercedes.

"You have a surveillance camera aimed at your own family?" Did Max think he needed to keep an eye on his family, or was this some kind of setup? He was a supposed computer whiz—he could have faked a video incriminating someone else.

"It's not aimed *at* them. I have a lot of expensive computer equipment in the cottage, so I have cameras aimed in all directions in case someone breaks in. Then I'd have evidence to give to the police. Unfortunately, I see a lot of things I'd rather not see. Like Julie and Brian in the field. It's disgusting." Max made a face. "And Evie with her midnight offerings."

"Midnight offerings?"

"Yeah, not sure what she does out there in the full moon, but it's creepy."

Images of Evie in a hooded cloak, worshipping the full moon, came to mind. I wasn't surprised—the girl looked as if she could be into something strange. But what about Josie? Could she have been involved in her mother's death? Or did she just have somewhere to go?

"This doesn't really prove anything. Maybe Josie had an appointment or was meeting someone. Just because she went out that morning doesn't mean she killed your grandmother."

"That's true, but if that were the case, then why did she lie?"

"She lied?"

Max nodded. "Aunt Marion's shrieks brought the whole family to Gram's room. We called the ambulance. While we were waiting, I noticed Josie wasn't there. Which was a little odd because she usually doesn't get up until noon. We thought maybe she didn't hear the commotion, so Evie went down to her room, but she wasn't there. Then the EMTs came and things got crazy. They worked on Gram for a while, but she was already gone." Max's voice broke, and he looked away.

"That must have been hard," I said.

He sniffed and swiped his nose with the sleeve of his hoodie. "Anyway, as they were leaving, Josie came sauntering down the hall in her bathrobe. She acted surprised about Gram, but I don't think she really was. She claimed she wasn't in her room, as she'd fallen asleep in the library, and you can't hear a thing that is going on in the house from in there, so we all believed her. It wasn't until a few days later that I got the idea to look at the surveillance videos from that morning. I don't usually look at them at all but wanted to see them bringing Gram out. Anyway, imagine my surprise when I rewound it a bit and saw Josie leaving in her car earlier that morning." He tapped on the lower right corner of the video. "See, it's time-stamped."

"Hmm. I see." He did have a point. Why would Josie lie if she was innocent? "But *why* would she want to kill your grandmother?"

"I'm not sure. She's not very stable, if you ask me. I know Gram wasn't too happy with her. Maybe she was afraid Gram was going to cut her out of the will or something."

"Was she?" I cut my eyes over to Adelaide, who shook her head.

Max shrugged. "If she was, no one said anything to me."

"Did Josie or anyone mention a recipe book?"

"Recipe book? No. We have a cook, so no one needs recipes. Well, Brian tried to cook dinner for

Julie once, but he set the smoke detectors off." Max shifted on his feet. "What have you found in your investigation?"

"My investigation? Umm ... well, I haven't found out much yet." If I kept him thinking that I was investigating Adelaide's death, his information might help me get the recipe book. "But thank you for coming to me with this. I'm sure it will help."

"Right. Well, if you need my help again, here's my cell number." Max handed me a piece of paper then left.

I stared after him as he closed the door. It was certainly a change of heart after his angry reaction at finding me at the cottage, but maybe I'd taken him by surprise last night. He did say he'd checked into me. He probably discovered I had an aptitude for solving murders, and since he already had suspicions about it himself, he just assumed I was looking into Adelaide's death. Though it did seem odd he would turn in his own family. Was it possible he had something to do with Adelaide's murder and he was trying to throw me off track?

"Max didn't have anything to do with my death. I told you he's a good boy," Adelaide said. Could she read my mind?

"Is he telling the truth? Was Josie not there when you were discovered?"

"I don't know. When I woke up, I was on the mortician's table. I doubt my own daughter would try to kill me, but I was so very sleepy that night, and when I woke up, my head felt heavy, so I think someone did ..."

"And what about *Betty's Recipes*? What does that have to do with any of this?"

Adelaide scrunched her brows together. "Surely you know how important recipes are."

"You said it was in the daisy patch. Did you mean the one in front of the cottage where Max has his computers?"

"Daisy patch? What are you talking about? I never said that. I said it was with Daisy...but now I'm not sure. It seems everything has been moved around. Someone has been messing with my things."

Great. I was no closer than before to finding the book, and now I had a potential recipe-book-stealing-killer to deal with. "So where do you suggest I look, then?"

"I'm not really sure. But I know you will figure it out. You have a knack for these things."

I opened my mouth to ask more questions, but Adelaide cut me off. "Oh, by the way, your grandmother dropped by to visit me, and she's doing great in the afterlife. She said to tell you that you were doing a good job and she's very proud of you."

"Really?" My eyes stung. I'd seen quite a few ghosts since I'd gotten this rare ability, but never once had Gram come to me. Even though she was the one ghost I would've loved to speak with. The thought that she was doing well and watching over me from beyond warmed my heart.

"Yes indeed. And she wanted me to remind you not to forget to believe in magic." And then Adelaide disappeared before I could ask any more questions about her killer, the recipe book, or my grandmother.

Chapter 13

Later that day, I was crouched in the art aisle, trying to stuff a tall book into the bottom bookshelf, my leg cramping somewhat from the effort, when the bell over the door chimed and a familiar voice called out from the front room.

"I'm baa-ack..."

"Pepper!" I shoved the book into place and darted out front.

Pepper was standing in the doorway, her red hair pulled into a tight chignon at the base of her neck, one long strand falling down beside her oval face. Her pink T-shirt and black yoga pants with matching pink stripes on the sides were just loose enough to be tasteful while still showing off her slim figure. In her left hand, she balanced a silver tray complete with coffeepot, cups and saucers, and a crystal creamer and sugar bowl. A doily-covered plate loaded with scones rested beside the teapot.

I rushed over and took the tray, setting it on the coffee table and giving her a hug. "How was your trip?"

"It was great. You know I love to see the family." We sat on the sofa, and Pepper busied herself pouring coffee and putting the scones on little white napkins. "How are things here?"

"Oh, nothing new here. A ghost appeared and wanted me to find some weird book, and then I find out she's been murdered. The usual stuff."

Pepper laughed then turned somber. "Wait, that means someone died. Who was it?"

"Adelaide Hamilton."

Pepper nibbled her scone thoughtfully. "I remember her. I didn't know her well. So her ghost contacted you?"

"Yes." It felt wonderful to finally be able to talk to someone about Adelaide's ghost. Pepper was the only one who knew I talked to dead people. It wasn't exactly something I wanted to be public knowledge.

We sipped the coffee and nibbled the scones while I told her the whole story, starting from Adelaide's appearance at her own wake and ending with Max's video and his suspicions of his grandmother being murdered.

"What do Gus and Striker say about her murder?"

"Gus seemed convinced it was natural causes the other day, but something must've happened in the meantime. Otherwise why would Striker have been at the Hamilton mansion at night?"

Pepper shrugged. "Well, he could have just been patrolling like he said. Maybe he saw your car and followed you. How are things between the two of you, anyway?"

Good question. "Things are okay. It does kind of put a damper on dating when a ghost keeps popping up everywhere."

Pepper laughed and settled back in the couch. "Well, then I guess you'll just have to do what you need to do to get rid of her. So I assume you're investigating? What have you found?"

I shook my head. "I'm not investigating her murder. Adelaide never asked me to. She just wanted me to find the book."

Pepper squinted at me as though she had a headache. "What book?"

"Some recipe book. Weird thing is that Gram actually mentioned the book in her will. Wanted to make sure it got to Elspeth, but I never found it in her belongings."

Pepper's face turned serious. She put her coffee cup down, spilling a little bit of mocha-colored liquid onto the white saucer. "Did you say *recipe* book?"

"Yeah, it was a friend of theirs, Betty. Must have some really good recipes in it."

Peppers eyes widened. "Betty's recipes?"

"Yeah. You've heard of it?"

"My grandmother mentioned it..." Pepper's voice trailed off. Pepper had always said her grandmother was magic. In fact, that's where she had gotten her recipes for the special teas she made, which she claimed could produce enchanting results. And it wasn't just the herbs she used—Pepper claimed to have inherited certain spiritualistic gifts that she used to infuse the tea. She'd been making magic tea since we were kids, and I'd often brushed them off as fanciful...but lately I'd come to realize that maybe Pepper's teas really did have something special to them. If Pepper's grandmother had mentioned *Betty's Recipes*, the book might contain more than just your average recipes for breads and stews.

"You don't mean..." I couldn't bring myself to say it, but it made sense with everything that was going on. I should've thought of it before—why would a ghost care about a book? Only one reason. That book was important. Even my own grandmother had mentioned it in her will.

"That's not a book of recipes, Willa. That book is a spell book."

"*Meow!*" Pandora came trotting out from the back room and rubbed her head against Pepper's leg while I absorbed the information. Of course it was a book of spells—why else would it be so important? I'd known there had to be more to it. But spells? My grandmother hadn't been involved with spells, had she? I thought about Adelaide's recent message from my grandmother—she'd said "don't forget to believe in magic."

The practical side of me wanted to scoff that there was no such thing as a spell book, but seeing as I talked to ghosts, I could hardly just dismiss the idea of mysticism and magic. It didn't matter anyway—whether the book was full of recipes for spells or not, I still had to find it.

"No matter what's in that book, I need to find it, or Adelaide is going to keep popping up and ruining my dates with Striker."

"But now it may be more complicated than you thought. I mean, if it really is a spell book, others will be after it."

"And it might give someone motive to kill Adelaide ... but why kill her now?"

Pepper shrugged. "Maybe they got tired of waiting. You did say that her cancer was in remission. Maybe whoever it was got frustrated and decided to take a chance."

"So someone in Adelaide's house might want the spell book for themselves? Like a witch?"

"Yeah, and not the good kind, either." Pepper's emerald eyes darkened. "If Adelaide had the book in her care, then she was one of the good guys. Like your grandmother and mine. But if someone killed her to get it, then that person would want to use the spells for evil intent."

"*Meow!*" Pandora jumped up on the coffee table.

"Hey, that's not polite." I shooed her away, and she hopped down reluctantly, leaving a deep scratch mark with her claw. I could have sworn she smirked over her shoulder at me as she trotted back to her cushion in the window.

"But which one is it?" I wondered. "Josie was leaving in the car that morning. Did she kill her mother and then take the book somewhere? Or maybe it was Evie...Max said she did creepy things under the full moon. But then it could also be Max trying to throw us off track."

"It could be any of them or all of them," Pepper said. "We don't know if Adelaide was killed or if the book has already fallen into wicked hands. You still need to make an attempt to find it and get it to Elspeth."

"And one way to do that would be to find Adelaide's killer."

"*Mew!*" Pandora lay with her paws curled in front of her and her tail swishing behind her as she listened to our conversation, giving the impression that she actually knew what we were saying.

"I need to go back into the Hamiltons'. I think I might have been onto something in the library, but I doubt they are going to let me in again."

"Now *that*," Pepper said as she piled the teacups, napkins, and other items onto the tea tray, "I can help you with. I haven't paid my respects yet, and I'm sure I should bring them a soothing tea. One that might give them loose lips and cause them to blurt out the truth. You can come with me."

"Okay." My voice rose an uncertain octave at the end of the word. It wasn't that I didn't want to go with Pepper, but her teas ... well, as I said, I had come to believe there was something about them. It was just unfortunate that they often backfired. I was worried about what a tea that was supposed to give people loose lips would actually do.

Pepper neatly placed the last napkin on the tray and then leaned back on the couch with a smirk on her face. "So you believe in this stuff now, don't you?"

Pepper got a kick out of the fact that I resisted believing in magic despite the fact that I talked to ghosts. But now, I was starting to be a little more open minded. There were a lot of things going on that could only be explained away with magic. But I didn't need to admit that to Pepper. She'd just gloat. "Maybe. Maybe not."

"Huh." She hefted the tray and stood. "Well, I better be getting back to my shop. Do you want to go to the Hamiltons' tomorrow around noon? I can get Camilla to watch the store."

"Sounds good."

"*Meeoo!*" Pandora chimed in.

"No, you can't come."

Pandora arched her back and hissed then spun around in her bed, curling up with her nose tucked under her tail and her back to me.

Pepper laughed as she opened the door. "I see she hasn't changed. If only she knew she's much better off staying here. Our visit tomorrow could be dangerous, especially if one of the Hamiltons turns out to be a cold-blooded killer."

Chapter 14

The next morning, the bookstore was busy with customers. I made a tidy sum on a first edition of *The Cat Who Could Read Backwards* and sold dozens of other books for more modest sums. I didn't have much time to think about the Hamiltons or which one of them was a killer. For all I knew, they'd all been in on it together.

It all made perfect sense now. Even though Gus had claimed that Adelaide died of natural causes, Max's suspicions and what Adelaide herself had said combined with the fact that Striker had been nosing around the Hamilton estate all led in the same direction—murder.

It was funny, though. Gus usually didn't lie to me to keep me from investigating murders. Maybe she was trying a new tactic to keep me away. I guessed I'd have the last laugh, since it didn't work.

Too bad I hadn't had a chance to try to use my powers of persuasion to extract information from Striker. He'd been suspiciously absent. I hadn't even gotten a how-you-doing text from him. I had to admit that I'd harbored a secret hope that he would show up at my house for dinner the previous night, but the only thing I had found on my doorstep was a red-and-white-checkered-cloth-covered picnic basket that held the most delicious beef stew and biscuits from Elspeth. She even included a piece of her mouthwatering apple pie and a little handmade treat for Pandora along with a note in her scrawling handwriting stating it was one of her favorite dishes but she hoped she'd gotten the recipe correct.

Was the mention of the word "recipe" a coincidence? I wondered how much Elspeth actually knew about the recipe book. Gram had said I should give it to Elspeth. If it was a spell book, wouldn't Elspeth know that? Maybe Elspeth knew about magic and all her "lucky guesses" weren't really guesses at all.

Before I had any more time to think about Elspeth, Pepper appeared, carrying the pink-and-green quilted tea cozy bag she had custom-made specifically to keep the water warm in her teapot. It also had sections for scones, tea, sugar, and milk. It was her own mobile tea shop.

I eyed the bag warily as we drove to the Hamilton mansion. "Is the loose-lip tea in there?"

Pepper smiled. "Hopefully. I also infused it with a droning charm. Whoever drinks the tea will drone on and on without noticing what's going on around them. I figured I could keep the Hamiltons busy with that while you slip out and check the library."

The mansion looked more imposing today than it had on my previous visit. Perhaps it was because I now knew that a murderer lived inside. Pepper ascended the granite steps with her quilted bag slung over her shoulder and knocked on the wooden door. The butler—I remembered his name was John from the other day—opened it, raising a brow at Pepper and then looking down his nose at me.

"Did you leave something here the other day?" he asked.

"She's with me. I've come to pay my respects. I brought a special herbal tea for the family." Pepper held up the bag and gave him her sweetest smile. Obviously he was a lot more taken with her than he had been with me, because he opened the door wide and said, "Of course. Come right in."

Pepper breezed in, and he smiled as she passed him, then his smile snapped into a frown as he looked at me with my right foot tentatively poised over the threshold. "I suppose you can come in, too."

We followed him down the hall to the same room where I'd talked to the family the other day. Josie was the only one there today. She wore faded jeans and a white silk blouse and was slumped on the off-white linen sofa looking as if she were almost asleep.

"Ahem." John cleared his throat.

Josie jerked awake with a half snore and looked at us with bleary eyes. "Wha?"

"You have visitors," the butler said then did his disappearing act.

Pepper sat beside Josie, taking her hand. "I'm so sorry for your loss. I'm Pepper St. Onge, from The Tea Shoppe downtown."

"Yes, of course." Josie's eyes drifted to the bag.

"I brought tea." Pepper opened the bag and produced a silver trivet, which she placed on the coffee table. Then she reached in and pulled out a matching silver teapot and put that gently on top of the trivet. She proceeded to reach in several more times, coming up with embroidered napkins, cups and saucers, matching silver creamer and sugar, a doily-covered plate, and an assortment of scones.

Josie watched as if mesmerized. I couldn't really blame her. She was probably wondering, as I was, how Pepper fit all that stuff in the small bag. It reminded me of those small cars at the circus that an impossible number of clowns pile out of.

"I brought enough for everyone," Pepper said, looking around the room. "Where are the other Hamilton family members?"

Josie looked up as if just noticing no one else was in the room. She waved her hand. "Oh, they're around somewhere."

Pepper cast a glance at me, and I shrugged.

"Well, I'm sure you'll like this tea. I created it specifically to help with grief," Pepper said as she handed the steaming cup to Josie.

Josie took a tentative sip, her red lipstick marring the rim of the white porcelain teacup. She frowned, swirling the liquid around her mouth, and then swallowed. "Oh, it's quite good."

We sipped and nibbled politely while Pepper soothed Josie with simple questions. I only pretended to drink the tea. I wasn't sure if it really worked, but I wasn't taking any chances on getting "loose lips." I did notice that Josie became more talkative as time passed. Was the tea really working, or was she just finally starting to wake up from the nap we'd obviously interrupted?

"It must have been awful finding your mother like that," Pepper said.

Josie nodded. "A terrible shock."

"It's bad enough when your parent passed, but to be the one to find them..." Pepper soothed.

"Yes ... Oh, I didn't find Mom," Josie said. "Aunt Marion did."

"It's still awful. I'm sure you had to see her."

Josie's eyes welled and took on a faraway look. "No, I was asleep in the library."

Pepper slid her eyes over to me. Josie was lying.

"Well, it must be nice to have such a close family and have had everyone around you that morning," Pepper continued her covert interrogation.

Josie snorted. "Close? They're a bunch of vipers. They were all only here because they are living off Mom's money."

"Oh, well, I'm sure there's plenty to go around," I said.

"Pfft." Josie sipped more tea. "Not if you ask Lisa. She doesn't think there is enough for her. And my brother, well, he won't say boo to his wife. Who knows what Max is up to, always lurking around, and I can't believe he talked Mom into letting him use the cottage. What does he do out there? We have a lot of old family stuff out there, and I don't like the idea of him fooling around with it."

"Evie and Julie must have liked being so close to their grandma, though," I said.

Josie's face relaxed into a smile. "Yes, my two girls were very precious to Mom. The girls are so different from each other. Did you know they were twins?"

I nodded. "Yep. Seems they do a lot together."

Except worship the moon in the middle of the night—only Evie does that.

Josie bit her lip. "They did until Julie hooked up with Brian. Oh, he seems nice enough, very interested in family gatherings and the Hamilton history, but I can tell Evie doesn't like him."

"Maybe she's jealous that Julie has found someone and she's a third wheel," Pepper said.

Josie frowned. "That's probably it. She doesn't seem interested in finding anyone of her own, though. More interested in sleeping in late and reading. Evie and Mom were the closest..." Josie's voice trailed off, and she picked a scone off the tray. "These are good. Cranberry?"

"Yes, my grandmother's recipe," Pepper said. "I suppose your family had some great old recipes."

"Recipes? Mom hasn't baked in years. Evie wanted her to teach her, but the lessons didn't take. We have a cook, so why is baking necessary?"

"Good point." Pepper poured more tea into Josie's cup, and the conversation turned to more mundane matters. Josie talked a lot but seemed introspective, as if she were paying little attention to the two of us in the room with her. Was Pepper's droning charm taking effect?

I put my full teacup down on the saucer. "May I use your bathroom?"

Josie waved her hand in the air, barely acknowledging my question. "Whatever."

I slipped out the door into the hall and managed to get into the library unnoticed. Now what? I couldn't shake the feeling that there was something important in the library, but where? Was the recipe book in here? There were hundreds of books. It would take me forever to search the entire room.

"Adelaide?" I whispered. No such luck. Ghosts rarely turned up when you wanted them to.

My eyes fell on the daisy painting. I had been interrupted before when I was searching for the recipe book on the shelves underneath—maybe I should start there. Just as I got to the painting, though, I heard a noise in the hallway.

Someone was coming!

I didn't want to be caught snooping in the library again, so I slipped into the reading nook and plastered myself against the wall behind the burgundy velvet drape. I held my breath as I heard someone coming into the room. Then I heard strange clanking and scratching sounds. I risked peeking and was surprised to see Lisa take a silver candlestick off the fireplace mantel and drop it into an oversized burlap tote bag, where it clanked against whatever else was in there. She turned, pressing her index finger to her lips, her eyes lighting up as she spied something on the other side of the room. I ducked back behind the curtain as she made a beeline in that direction.

"What are you doing?" A male voice sounded from the direction of the doorway.

"Nothing." Lisa, defiant. "Not that it's any of your business anyway, Brian."

"It looks like you're stealing stuff," Brian said.

"I'm not stealing. I'm collecting things to sell. We have too much stuff, the house is loaded, and we need to pare down a bit, don't you think?"

"No. I don't. This stuff isn't yours to sell off at some auction."

"I'm not taking it to *some auction*. Felicity Bates has expressed an interest in buying some of our family things. She's especially interested in these books here. She's a collector."

"I don't care what she is. I don't think you should be selling anything. This is for the family to decide on."

Lisa snorted. "Well, since you aren't family, I guess you can butt out."

Lisa and Brian continued arguing, but I had stopped listening as soon as I'd heard the name

Felicity Bates. The mere mention of the woman made me shudder. She was bad news, as I'd found out quite painfully when I'd first moved to Mystic Notch. Rumor had it she was some kind of a witch, and witches used spell books. She was no book collector. She was after *Betty's Recipes*.

Marion's harsh voice interrupted my thoughts. "What are you people doing in here?"

I shrank back farther into the nook.

"Lisa was stealing things and putting them in this bag," Brian said.

"Stealing? You put those back." I heard scraping and clanking sounds, which I assumed was Lisa putting the things back, and then Marion said, "Now get out of here, both of you. There'll be no more stealing or appropriating of goods. These are all Hamilton family heirlooms, and neither one of you is welcome to them."

I could hear the sounds of Marion herding Lisa and Brian out of the room. I wanted to go back over to the painting and look for the book. I was sure it must still be here somewhere. Otherwise Felicity Bates wouldn't be trying to get Lisa to sell the books to her. But I didn't dare stay in the room any longer. I'd already been gone for quite some time, and I was afraid that even with the droning charm Josie might notice how long I'd been missing. I couldn't run the risk of the Hamiltons becoming more suspicious of me. I might need them to answer questions later on.

As I slipped out of the library, a dark figure at the end of the hall caught my eye. Evie. She narrowed her eyes in an accusatory glare.

I waved cheerfully. "I was just looking for the bathroom. Wrong turn."

I scurried back to the drawing room to collect Pepper and get the heck out of there.

Chapter 15

"Did you find what you were looking for?" Pepper asked as we pulled out of the Hamilton driveway.

"No, but I discovered something disturbing."

"What?"

"Felicity Bates approached Lisa Hamilton, wanting to buy things from the house—including books."

"Oh boy, this can't be good."

"Tell me about it. Felicity is bad news."

"No, not that." Pepper nodded her chin toward the side-view mirror. "That."

Striker's car was coming up the road very quickly behind me.

Was he pulling me over? He didn't have his lights on, but by the way he was advancing on me, it sure seemed that way. I pulled to the side of the road, and to my dismay he stopped behind me. I hesitated, watching him open his door.

Pepper shoved my arm. "Well, get out there and see what he wants."

I got out, walking the length of the Jeep to meet him in the middle. My heart did a little two-step at the way his tall, broad-shouldered frame filled out his uniform. I'd seen him in it many times before, but for some reason he still had this effect on me. Guess I'm a sucker for a man in uniform. He looked a little tired, with a shadow of stubble that I itched to run my fingertips across.

"Please tell me you didn't pull me over for speeding," I said.

Striker grinned. "You? Never. I noticed you're getting awfully friendly with the Hamiltons."

"Not really. Pepper needed to pay her respects, and she wanted company. I haven't talked to them other than the two times I came here." I decided to keep Max's visit to myself. After all, he did offer to help me and asked me not to tell the police about his suspicions. Okay, that in itself was kind of weird, but I hadn't decided yet if he was a suspect or an ally, and I didn't want to say a thing to Striker until I was sure.

"And the time you were skulking around over at the cottage," Striker reminded me.

I wanted to come up with a pithy answer, but a swirling mist on my right distracted me. I blinked, hoping it was just something in my eye.

"Something wrong with your eye?"

"No." My reply had a tinge of irritation, but it wasn't aimed at Striker. As I'd feared, the swirling mist was Adelaide's ghost. Why did she have to show up now? Couldn't she have shown up when I was in the house and needed her guidance to find the book?

"The book's not in the house, I don't think," Adelaide said. I raised a brow in her direction.

"Is there something over there?" Striker asked, a curious look on his face as he glanced in Adelaide's direction. For a split second I feared he could see her, because his brows snapped together, but then his eyes jerked over to some spot behind my left shoulder.

I turned to look, but nothing was there. "Did you see something?" I asked.

"No."

"Me either."

"I had that book carefully hidden, but now all my things are rearranged. Someone has been going through them," Adelaide continued.

"Lisa," I blurted out.

Striker scrunched up his face. "Who?"

"Oh, nothing. Sorry." I shifted my stance so that Adelaide was behind me then focused on Striker. "So did you want something?"

"I haven't seen you in a while, and I wanted to catch up." Striker waved his hand in the air as if waving something away, and I looked behind me again. What was wrong with him?

"You wanted to catch up out here in the middle of the road?" I asked. Now that I knew Adelaide had been murdered, I was positive Striker was investigating the case. Why wouldn't he just tell me that? I pushed down a flutter of annoyance. He was always telling me not to butt in as if I were some bumbling idiot that didn't know how to investigate a murder. He seemed to have forgotten that I was once a top-notch crime journalist in Massachusetts. "Or were you trying to figure out what I knew about Adelaide's murder?"

Striker's eyes snapped from the place beyond my shoulder to my face. "Murder? What are you talking about? I told you she wasn't murdered."

So he was going to play dumb. Well, two could play at that game. I wasn't going to give him any of the information I'd gleaned. Not that it was much. "You just happened to see me driving here and pulled me over, then?"

Striker leaned forward and straightened my shirt collar, muddying my thoughts. "Yes. We haven't seen each other in a while, and I meant to ask you to dinner, but Gus is short-handed, so I've been working a shift here in Mystic Notch as well as my regular shift over in Dixford Pass and…" He frowned at something to the left of me, and for a minute I was afraid he could see Adelaide, but her ghost had drifted out from behind me on the right and was now intent on distracting me.

"You shouldn't be wasting time here with *your* guy. I need you to find that book so I can get together with *my* guy." Her eyes turned dreamy. "And I feel that he's close. Very close. But if you don't find the book soon, I may lose him forever."

I glanced over at her and noticed something interesting in the woods. I could just barely make it out through the misty shimmer of her body. At the very edge of the Hamilton property, the pine trees grew thick, but there appeared to be a clearing about twenty feet in. Inside the clearing were large slate stones. Gravestones. The Harrington family plot. And in the middle I could see an old vine-covered structure. The mausoleum. Would that be a good place to hide a book?

"So you wanna get together later tonight?" Striker asked.

I jerked my eyes back in his direction.

"You don't have time. You have to find the book," Adelaide said.

"Umm ... I do, but I have some work to catch up on."

Disappointment flashed in his eyes. "Ok. I better get back to work, myself. Maybe later this week?"

The hopeful look in his eye twisted my heart. "Definitely later."

I really wanted to get together sooner rather than later, but it was hard to concentrate with Adelaide floating around. She was right—I did have to find the book soon. Once I did, she could be reunited with her husband, and I could concentrate on my relationship with Striker. Not to mention that the book would then be safe from those who wanted to use it with bad intent.

***

I made it back to the bookstore with a tuna sub in my hand shortly after lunch. Pandora didn't bother to greet me. She was probably mad I'd gone off to Hamiltons without her.

I pinched some tuna out of the sub and put it on a little plate for her as a peace offering. She sniffed the air then favored me with a haughty look before stretching her legs out in front of her and erupting in a sharp-toothed yawn. She then hopped out of her bed, trotted over to the tuna, and ate it without giving me another look.

With all my extracurricular activities at the Hamilton mansion, I'd gotten behind in cataloguing new books. I'd picked up several lots of old leather-bounds at a local estate sale, and they were waiting to be put into the system and displayed on the shelves. I hefted a big box onto the counter and got to work.

I wasn't at it for more than ten minutes when the door burst open and Gus stormed in. She stopped short in front of the counter and stared at me, her hands on her hips. Her long blond hair was pulled up into a tight bun, the way she always wore it when she was on duty. I figured she thought it made her look like a tough sheriff, but it was kind of hard to look tough when you had a petite hourglass figure, even if it was stuffed into a plain brown sheriff uniform. Her face was pinched into an angry scowl.

"I've been getting complaints about you from the Hamilton family," she said.

I feigned innocence. "You have?"

"Yes. They said you've been hanging around, asking questions. This isn't a murder investigation, Willa. And even if it was, you wouldn't be a part of it."

I pressed my lips together and wondered just who had called the police on me. "Really? Who said I was hanging around? I've only been there twice. The other day I went to pay my respects for Gram, and this morning Pepper wanted company when she went to pay hers."

"Never mind who called me. I want you to leave that family alone. Adelaide was not murdered."

"Really? Then why did you bring in Striker?"

"What are you talking about? I didn't bring in Striker, because there is no probable cause, therefore, no investigation. Why do you ask that?"

I decided to keep my mouth shut. I wasn't sure why Gus would be lying to me about Adelaide's murder. It didn't make much sense, as word of her investigation was sure to get out on the Mystic Notch grapevine sooner or later. She and Striker had never purposely kept the fact that they were investigating a murder from me before. Odd that they would hide it now, but if she was going to be that way, I wouldn't volunteer anything either.

"I'm sorry there was a misunderstanding with the Hamiltons. It won't happen again," I said to appease her.

"It better not—" Gus's phone chirped, and her eyes snapped down to her belt, where the phone was secured. Her brow creased slightly. "Gertie Sloan? I better get this."

She snapped the phone off her belt and turned her back to me as if she wanted privacy. A polite person would've gone on with their work, trying not to eavesdrop, but I wasn't that polite. Gertie was the county medical examiner, and if she was calling Gus, I knew it had to be something good. I leaned forward, tilting my head so as to best hear the conversation.

"Excessive amounts of opiates?" Gus said. "How did you even..."

"But there was no autopsy on Adel—" Gus bit off her words and glanced back in my direction. I jerked my head down at the paperwork, hoping she wouldn't notice I had been eavesdropping. She stepped farther away and continued talking. "On her. So how did you find out what was in her bloodstream?"

"From Blakes ... for the cause of death... Oh, I see. Well, that is unusual and disturbing."

Another glance back at me while she listened to Gertie on the other end.

"Right. Too bad she's already been buried. Thanks for letting me know. Yes, I know, probable cause and all that, but let's hope it doesn't come to exhumation." She snapped the phone shut and whirled around to face me. "Were you listening?"

"No, not me. I was cataloguing books." I pointed to the stack of books.

"Good. You can forget about hearing any of that. It had nothing to do with you." She turned and strode to the door, ripping it open then turning back to me. "And stay away from the Hamiltons."

I watched her leave, wondering what exactly the call had been about. From what I could gather, somebody's blood had too many opiates in it. Opiates could knock someone out and render them unconscious. And why would someone want to render someone else unconscious? One reason could be so they could easily kill them in their bed and make it look as if they died in their sleep.

If my guess was correct, that call had been about Adelaide Hamilton. But Gus's surprise had been obvious. She hadn't known about any foul play before Gertie's call. But if that were true, then why had Striker *already* been investigating the case?

***

Eddie Striker stared down at the phone in his hand. Adelaide Hamilton had been murdered? He had a hard time believing it, but the information Gus had just given him left little question. As part of a new state initiative to gather information on infections that were now so prevalent in the elderly, the funeral director had sent a sample of Adelaide's blood off to be inspected. Since there had been no sign of foul play, the lab had taken their time, and Adelaide's memorial service had gone on as planned.

Adelaide didn't have C-diff or any of the other dreaded infections, but the test revealed her blood had a high amount of opiates. Okay, not so suspicious considering she had cancer, but Gus had verified with her doctor that the cancer was in remission, and though he'd been refilling her prescriptions, Adelaide wasn't in pain and not taking many pain pills, if any.

Upon hearing this news, the funeral director mentioned something disturbing to Gus. He'd noticed bruises on the side of Adelaide's mouth. Broken blood vessels in her eyes. All signs of being suffocated. However, he had assumed she'd been in the last throes of cancer. He'd seen the bodies of many cancer victims, and they were in much worse states, so he didn't think much about it when he'd prepared her.

Striker remembered Willa accusing him of investigating Adelaide's murder. He had thought it was strange at the time since there was no murder. Did Willa know something that he and Gus didn't? It would be just like her to try to track down the killer herself. She had a habit of doing that. That would explain why he kept finding her skulking around the Hamiltons'. But *why* would someone want to murder Adelaide?

"That's a good question." Louis Hamilton's ghost appeared in the passenger seat of Striker's police car, practically giving him a heart attack.

"Do you have to pop up unannounced like that?"

"Sorry. I don't know how to announce myself. I can't believe what I just heard you say on the phone. My Adelaide murdered? By whom?"

"I wish I knew. But since she was found at home in bed, it looks like it was probably one of your relatives."

Louis frowned. "Gosh, that's hard to believe. It wouldn't be one of my offspring." His face brightened. "Maybe it was that Lisa or Marion. I never did like Marion, always poking into our affairs, but Adelaide wouldn't let me turn her out. Twins have a very close relationship."

"So you don't have any idea who it would have been? You're not much help. In fact, you're getting in the way. What was that business outside of the Hamilton ... err ... your mansion earlier today? Couldn't you see I was talking to Willa?" Striker asked.

"Oh, sorry about that. I just sensed that Adelaide was so close, and you're not doing nearly enough to find that book. I had to pop in and give you some instructions."

"More like distractions. It's hard to pay attention to you when I'm trying to be talking to humans who don't know you exist."

"Well, that's just too bad, young man. Can't you find that book any quicker? I feel my Adelaide is slipping away ..."

Louis's voice sounded so sad that Striker almost felt sorry for him. Almost. But the fact was, he felt as if his relationship with Willa was slipping away, too. And it was all because of Louis. "Yeah, this isn't good for either one of our love lives. So what were these instructions you were going to give me? Do you know where the book is?"

"I don't know where it is, but I have some suggestions as to where to look. We always joked that Adelaide was forgetful. She'd hide things and not be able to find them again. So for anything important, she'd pick a Hamilton ancestor and hide it near them."

"What do you mean *near* them?"

"The Hamilton line goes way back, and we have a lot of family heirlooms and memorabilia. Aunt Lottie's favorite rocking chair. Uncle Henry's beer stein. Old family portraits. She'd associate the item with an ancestor and hide it near their portrait or in one of their favorite things. One time she hid a necklace in the drawer of a side table that had a lamp that Aunt Cleo brought back from the Orient in the twenties. Another time a pocket watch she was planning to give me for Christmas went into a gravy boat my great-grandparents brought over from England."

"So what ancestor did she associate the book with?"

Louis grimaced. "*That*, I don't know."

"Well, that's hardly helpful."

"I suppose not, but I happen to know that Adelaide was meticulous about keeping the Hamilton heirlooms in order. She didn't like the house to be cluttered, though. So she donated a lot of stuff to the historical society. She used the stone cottage for storing and sorting those items. If someone in the family was out to kill her and Adelaide was worried about that recipe book, she might well have hidden the item in the cottage. It's worth a look, right?"

"I suppose it can't hurt." Striker remembered the last time he'd been at the cottage. Willa had been there, too. Coincidence? He also remembered how mad Max had gotten when he'd thrown them out. Was there something in there the boy didn't want him to see?

When he'd been there before, he hadn't been on police business. He'd been trying to get a handle on the family and figure out how he could get his hands on the book. Since he hadn't been on official business, he'd left when questioned. This time, it wouldn't be as easy to get rid of him. *Now,* in addition to his unofficial business of looking for the book, he had official business that would allow him to show his badge and search the premises—Adelaide's murder.

Chapter 16

I felt bad about lying to Gus. Well, technically I hadn't lied—I just didn't tell her everything I knew. Though the part about not going to the Hamiltons' house was probably a lie. I was sure I was going to end up there again sooner or later. But there was no way I could tell her that I'd talked to Adelaide's ghost and was looking for a book of spells. Gus was a total nonbeliever when it came to magic. I couldn't get judgmental on her about that, though. I'd been pretty much a nonbeliever most of my life, too.

Looking back, I wondered if Gram had tried to instill magic in me from early on. She always said I was special. Adelaide had even said Gram wanted her to give me the message to believe in magic, and Gram had mentioned *Betty's Recipes* in her will. If she'd known about the spell book, then surely she'd known about magic? And what about Elspeth? Elspeth was supposed to get the book. Did she know of magic too?

I'd always thought it was strange that Gram had left her house, her bookstore, and Pandora to me alone instead of splitting them between Gus and me. Since she'd left Gus a sum of money equal to what I'd inherited, I had assumed she was just trying to make it easy on us, so we didn't have to go through the work of splitting things up. But it was odd that she'd leave the property in Mystic Notch to me, because I'd lived in Massachusetts at the time of her passing. Wouldn't it have made more sense to leave the property to Gus, who already lived here? But now I wondered if it wasn't all part of a plan to get me to move back to Mystic Notch. And if that was the outcome Gram had wanted, then it had worked perfectly. But why would Gram have cared if I moved back after her death?

There didn't seem to be much reason for it. Maybe Gram knew all along I needed a change. I was happy here. I loved the bookstore and had made great friends. Friends who took care of me, like Elspeth with her homemade dinners. But if I didn't get that spell book, I was afraid things might change drastically, and not for the better. Maybe Elspeth would have some insight as to where Adelaide would have hidden it.

I still had Elspeth's basket and the—now clean—plates she'd left the previous night. What a great excuse to go to her house. I wasn't sure what I would ask her, but I hoped she'd have some insight into the Hamilton family dynamics or where

Adelaide might have kept the book. She'd known Adelaide—maybe she could point me in the right direction.

Pandora was more than happy to accompany me, and we made the short trek through the woods in record time. We split off in the clearing—Pandora heading toward the barn, and me heading to the front door.

I could smell the sugary scent of cookies as soon as I hit the first step. Elspeth was baking, and I hoped there was enough for me. As if on cue, she appeared in the doorway just as I raised my fist to knock.

"Oh, hi, Willa. Would you like to join me for some tea and cookies?" She held a tray in her hand. On it sat a round clear-glass pitcher swirling with amber liquid, a plate piled high with golden-yellow sugar cookies, and two cut-glass tumblers.

"I'd love to. Are you expecting someone else? I don't want to intrude." I eyed the two tumblers.

"Oh no, it'll just be us." She pushed the door open, and I set the basket down and then took the tray from her.

"I brought back your dishes from the other night. I really appreciate you sending supper over," I said.

"It's nothing, dear. I know you work long hours, and it's just as easy for me to cook for two and bring dinner over for you."

We settled into the white rocking chairs. Some of the pink roses had opened, and their papery floral scent perfumed the air. It was one of those pleasantly warm spring evenings that reminded me of the summer soon to come. The chirping of crickets, the angle of the setting sun, and the still air gave the evening a magical feel. Elspeth poured from the pitcher, the ice cubes clinking together like the bells of a wind chime.

"It's iced green tea." She handed me the cool glass, and I snagged a cookie from the plate.

"Delicious," I mumbled around a mouthful of cookie. The tea was earthy and sweet.

"Thanks." Elspeth sipped her drink. "Last time you were here, we were talking about Adelaide Hamilton. I don't suppose any of her family members consigned her recipe books to your bookstore, did they?"

"No, but I hear her daughter-in-law, Lisa, is in the market to sell some of the family belongings. I don't think she'll bring the books to me, though. I heard she was selling them to Felicity Bates."

Elspeth's eyes widened for a fraction of a second at the mention of Felicity. "Oh, really? I don't see why the Bates family would need any more things. They're quite wealthy themselves, and their mansion is stuffed to the gills."

"Tell me about it." I'd been inside the mansion, not that I wanted to remember. They certainly didn't need any of the Hamilton family items, but I suspected Felicity's offer to purchase was really a ploy to get her hands on the spell book.

Elspeth pressed her lips together. "Some members of Adelaide's family are not quite on the up and up, if you know what I mean. I don't think it's Lisa's place to be selling things off."

"It seems like a very unusual family dynamic over there. Did you know them well?"

"Not really. I knew Adelaide ages ago, like I told you before. And her husband, Louis, was quite a nice man. He died a long time ago. The kids were very young, and Adelaide never remarried." A smile flitted on Elspeth's lips. "True love, you know. Well, I don't need to tell you about true love."

My brows tugged together. "Huh?" Was she talking about Striker and me? I didn't think so—the way it was looking, we might not even get past "good friends," never mind true love.

Elspeth chuckled and took another sip of tea. "Anyway, I don't really know her children or grandchildren."

I ignored her "true love" comment. I had more important things on my mind than love. "What about Marion? You must've known her?"

"She was an odd duck. Never married or had children. Wasn't as outgoing as Adelaide but stuck to her like glue. Well, you know how sisters are—they have a special bond ... and since they were twins, it's even more special. Maybe I should go visit Marion. She must be feeling very upset. She used to like these raisin buns I made...oh, if only I had the recipe."

Was Elspeth hinting about that recipe book again? Now I *knew* she knew more about this than she was letting on, but I had no idea how to broach the subject with her. "Twins do seem to have a special bond."

Elspeth nodded.

"Like Hattie and Cordelia, and Adelaide has twin granddaughters, doesn't she?"

Elspeth frowned. "Different as night and day, I hear."

I wondered if Elspeth knew more about Evie than she was letting on. I remembered Max claiming his security footage caught Evie out in the moonlight. Was she a witch? Maybe Evie was after the spell book, too? Which reminded me—better get down to business fast.

"You don't have any idea where Adelaide would've put this recipe book, do you? I asked around for you when I was at the Hamilton mansion the other day, but no one seems to know anything about it," I said.

"I'm not sure, but sometimes people hide things right in plain sight."

My thoughts drifted to the library. I still couldn't shake the feeling that there was something important about that library, but my efforts to search it kept getting interrupted. But maybe the library was too obvious. "Did Adelaide have a favorite place on the property, or anyplace that was special to her?"

"Oh, yes. When she was dating Louis, they used to sneak off to the gardener's cottage and ... well, you know." Elspeth's eyes gleamed with mischief. "Back at the turn of the last century, the family had a full-time live-in gardener, if you can imagine that. But no one has lived in the cottage in a long time. After Louis died, Adelaide still loved to go there. She had it set up as a little retreat. Probably needed to get away from her nasty family. I hear her grandson is doing something with it now. I sure hope he hasn't changed that quaint little library."

"Library? There's a library in the cottage?"

"Oh, it's just a tiny thing, more like a reading nook, but Adelaide used to love to curl up right in the window seat and spend the afternoon reading. She was a big reader. In fact, she was one of your grandmother's better customers down at *Last Chance Books*."

"I didn't realize that," I said absently. My mind was still whirling about the fact that the cottage had a library. Maybe that was why she had mentioned the daisies. She hadn't hidden it in the library in the main house—she'd hidden it in the cottage. But why wouldn't she just say that?

I drained the rest of my tea glass and put it on the tray.

"How did you like the tea?" Elspeth asked.

"It was delicious."

"Good. It's one of Pepper's special blends."

I choked, my eyes darting to the empty glass. "That was one of Pepper's teas?"

Elspeth laughed. "Yes. Is there something wrong with that, dear?"

"No. It's just that sometimes her tea can have a strange effect." Maybe they weren't as potent when the tea was iced, I hoped.

Elspeth waved her hand in the air. "Oh, I know about Pepper's teas. They're just charming, aren't they?" She tapped the edge of her glass, which was still half full. "This one is a togetherness tea. And it seems to work, because I drank some earlier, and it brought you here, and we had this lovely conversation."

"Right." I doubted the tea had anything to do with my visit. I'd already planned to return her basket and plates from the night before. What worried me, though, was what effect the whole glass I drank might have on *me*. Would I suddenly be running into people I didn't want to see?

On the other hand, it might work to my benefit if it brought Adelaide's ghost around more to give me some direction. Then again, Pepper's teas often had the opposite effect of what she intended, so if the outcome was that Adelaide stayed away, then that would make my job much harder.

I'd already downed the drink, so there was no sense in taking up brain space worrying about it. I had more important things to think about, like making a plan to get back onto the Hamilton property and check out that stone cottage.

***

Inside Elspeth's barn, a shaft of moonlight pierced the darkness and beamed on the floor like a spotlight. Pandora trotted in, sitting just beside the illuminated area. Rustling noises came from behind the bales of hay and inside the stalls as the other cats padded out to greet her.

"We've heard that the evil one, Fluff, has an interest in this recipe book, and your human has yet to produce any satisfactory results." Inkspot jumped down from the hayloft, his sleek jet-black coat gleaming an inky indigo as he walked through the moonbeam of light. His rebuke made the hairs on Pandora's neck prickle, but she reined in her temper. Inkspot was the ruler, and she wouldn't be disrespectful.

"Fluff's interest is disturbing," Pandora purred. "But my human has made great strides. She thinks the book is in the Hamilton library."

"Well then, why doesn't she simply go and get it?" Otis preened his long whiskers with his paw.

"It's not that easy," Pandora said. "There are many Hamiltons in the house, and as you know, there is at least one in the home who wants to thwart our efforts."

"Is she sure it is there? If so, then you must work on her to figure out a way to get it." The Maine Coon, Kelley, swished her giant fluffy tail.

"Maybe we should get Elspeth involved," Ivy, a tan-and-black-striped Maine Coon, suggested.

"No!" Snowball's pure-white fur ruffled as she hissed the words. "Elspeth must never get in-

volved in these things. She must be protected at all costs."

The other cats murmured their agreement, and Ivy's white-ringed green eyes registered a flicker of contrition before she blinked them shut and shrank back into the corner. Pandora felt a pang of sympathy for her. She was one of the newer cats and still had a lot to learn.

Pandora had another morsel of information, and she sensed that now was the time to reveal it. "My human may not be retrieving the book as fast as you want, but she did come by some vital information."

Sasha raised a minky-brown brow, her ice-blue eyes showing interest. "And what might that be?"

A smug smile crept over Pandora's face. She relished being the center of attention with all eyes on her as she imparted important information that only she possessed. "The recipe book is not recipes for food, but rather recipes for charms and spells."

Otis snorted. "I figured that one out a long time ago. Of course it had to be a spell book. There wouldn't be such a big commotion over a simple recipe book." Leave it to Otis to rain on her parade.

Inkspot glared at him, and Pandora felt vindicated that their leader did not take kindly to the calico's sarcastic remark. "All the more serious, and all the more reason for us to work together." Inkspot turned back to Pandora. "What is your human's plan now?"

"She'll go back to the property to try to find it. She's made several attempts at searching the library, but I fear the book could be hidden anywhere on the property. It is large and could take a long time to search. Adelaide's ghost is very vague about where she has hidden it," Pandora said.

"Memory loss. The older humans all seem to have it. It takes a while for their ghosts to become clear." The tiger cat with a splash of a white chest and matching white on her paw tips, who was cursed with the unimaginative name of "Kitty", suggested.

"Not Elspeth," Tigger defended his mistress.

"No, she is special," Otis said. The rest of the cats nodded in agreement.

Inkspot moved into the center of the shaft of light and sat on his haunches to address the crowd. "It is time for us to help the humans now. We must help Willa locate the book. I need volunteers to travel to the Hamilton mansion by the light of the moon tomorrow night. We will use our seventh sense to home in on the location of the magical book. If it is truly a spell book, the vibration should be high, and our combined concentrations will allow us to pinpoint the location. But keep in mind, it may be dangerous. Fluff could be there. There could be others who wish harm on us."

"I'll go!"

"Me too!"

"Count me in!"

Meows came from every corner of the barn. All the cats volunteered. No one wanted to be left out of the special mission, no matter how dangerous.

Inkspot nodded his approval. "Very well, then." He turned to Pandora. "I'm afraid that may be the easy part. Once we know the location, the future of Mystic Notch will rest on your ability to steer Willa toward it."

Chapter 17

The next day, I saw Striker everywhere. I passed him in the morning on the way to the bookstore, I ran into him in *The Mystic Café*, where he was exiting as I was entering, and he was in front of me when I ran an errand to drop off books at the senior center. Not to mention that I thought I saw him drive past the bookstore more than once.

I hoped he wasn't following me, because I had big plans to scout out the cottage on the Hamilton estate, and I didn't want Striker around to spoil them.

After work, I went home and made a light supper of saltines, cottage cheese, and grape tomatoes with some hot sauce on top for added zip. It was all I had in the house. Then I changed into black pants, a black shirt, and a black hoodie. The perfect outfit for skulking around at night. Oddly enough, Pandora made no attempt to come with me when I finally left the house well after dark. Maybe she'd had enough adventuring for one week.

I drove my Jeep to the Hamilton mansion, killing the headlights when I got to the dirt road and then driving past the cottage and parking my Jeep farther down the road so that there was no way anyone would see it from driving by on the main road. If I got caught and someone called Gus, I was going to be in deep trouble with her. Not to mention Striker.

I hopped over the stone wall and skirted the tree line all the way up the road to the cottage. The moon was full, which helped to light my way but also made me easier to spot. I pulled the hood up to cover my face and hair. Should I have worn gloves? My pale hands glowed like luminescent beacons in the moonlight, and I shoved them into my pockets.

The night was too warm for the hoodie, but I needed it for cover. It was quiet out here in the middle of nowhere, the only sounds the chirping of crickets and the rustling of a few nocturnal animals. And an occasional meow. Wait? Meow? Were some of the feral cats out here? I hoped not. It was far from the shelter that we'd fashioned for them at the church, and I worried about mountain lions and bobcats.

I stopped across the street from the cottage. I could see a green glow in one of the windows. Otherwise, it was dark. Was Max in there?

My eyes drifted out over the field, where the occasional glow of a firefly sparked. The full moon hung high in the sky, splashing blue on the white petals of the daisies. Would Evie be out there tonight, practicing her spells or worshipping the moon or doing whatever it was she did in the middle of the night?

The amber glow of lights flickered in the Hamilton mansion. I wondered who was in there and what they were doing. Was Lisa skulking around, looking for items to sell to Felicity? Something outside the mansion caught my eye. Small, dark triangular shadows sticking up here and there. They looked almost like cat ears. Dozens of them. Moving through the field and surrounding the house. I blinked, and they were gone. Must have been my imagination. There was no way that many cats would be out in the field.

My eyes drifted back to the cottage. If the library was still in there and contained the spell book, maybe I could get Max to sell it to me. But first, I had to find out if the book was even in there.

A cloud drifted in front of the moon, and the night grew darker. It was now or never. I dashed across the street, wading through the tall grass and then dropping and rolling when I got to the daisy field.

When I was safe in the shadows of the cottage, I stood and brushed myself off, plastering my back against the cold stone wall and inching my way toward the corner of the house. Elspeth had said Adelaide like to curl up in the window seat in the cottage, and I had spotted a long, low window in the back that would be perfect for just that. If that was where the library was, I could peek inside and see if the book was there.

I slithered around the corner.

A strong arm grabbed me. Panic seized my heart as I was crushed against a muscular chest, a hand clamped over my mouth!

I struggled, kicking back with my feet until a familiar voice whispered in my ear, "Stop it. It's me."

Striker?

I stopped kicking, and he let go. I whirled to face him. "What are *you* doing here?"

He pushed the hood off my head and then looked me up and down, frowning at my all-black outfit. "I could ask you the same question."

There was barely an inch of space in between us. He must've just showered, because he smelled clean and musky. If it wasn't for the stern look on his face, I would've been tempted to kiss him. I debated what to tell him. Now that Gus's phone call had confirmed that Adelaide had been murdered, I could use that as an excuse for my snooping. I wouldn't have to tell him about Adelaide's ghost or the recipe book. He wouldn't like that I was messing around in his murder investigation, but it was better than the alternative.

"There's no use pretending," I said. "I know Adelaide was murdered. Gus was in my store when she got the phone call. So I got to thinking about who would've murdered her. Obviously a family member. And then I was wondering, why was Max out here that night? He lives in the converted stable with his parents. I want to check out the cottage, see what he's up to."

"That's trespassing."

"Are you going to arrest me? You obviously must suspect him, too, or you wouldn't be here investigating."

Striker's gaze dropped to my lips, and my heart flipped. Then he sighed and stepped away from me. "Fine. Let's go see what there is to see."

I didn't waste time being disappointed about the non-kiss or wondering why he had given in so easily. Normally he would have sent me packing, not teamed up with me. We crouched down and scuttled over to the low window. I poked my head up, my nose resting on the windowsill as I gazed around the eyelet-lace curtain into the room.

Shoot! It wasn't a library. It was a small country kitchen. The black-and-white-checked floor had seen better days, as had the scallop-trimmed, white-painted cupboards. The butcher-block counter held a variety of items. Green stoneware bowls, a clear glass pitcher, paper plates, take-out food boxes. But no recipe book.

"What are you doing here?" We spun around to see Max standing behind us. Where had he come from? I hadn't heard him come up. Clearly I needed to work on my snooping skills, because I hadn't noticed Striker lurking in the shadows either.

"We're jus—"

"Why did you tell him?" Max interrupted me, jerking his chin at Striker. "I told you not to bring the police in."

Striker slid his narrowed eyes over to me. "Tell me what, exactly?"

"I didn't tell him. He just showed up here," I said. "Anyway, you said I could come to you for help." Okay, a little bit of a lie—I wasn't technically coming to Max for help, but now that he was out here, maybe he *would* be helpful.

Max crossed his arms over his chest. "I said you could call my cell phone."

"Are you going to invite us in?" Striker asked.

"No."

"Why? Are you hiding something in there? I can come back with a warrant," Striker said.

Max sighed and unfolded his arms. "Fine. Come on in."

We followed him through the oak door with its rounded top, and I stopped short, staring at what was inside. I don't know what I expected. Probably a cozy furnished cottage. But it looked more like the computer lab of a high-tech company. The main area was one big room, with a big stone fireplace at one end and a doorway to the kitchen on the other. It was dark, save for the moon-and-stars screen savers on the three gigantic computer screens and a variety of red and green LED lights that blinked from the fronts of various pieces of computer equipment.

Striker rammed into me then caught me from falling on my face. He let out a low whistle as he looked around. "Wow, this place looks like NASA. What the heck do you do in here?"

Max shrugged. "The usual. Gaming. Programming."

Even someone not experienced in reading lies on people's faces could tell he was lying.

"So, hacking..." Striker said.

Max's face turned peevish. "Not maliciously..."

No wonder Max acted so strangely and didn't want the cops involved.

"Did your grandmother know about this?" I asked. "Did you fight about it?" Maybe Adelaide wasn't too happy about having illegal activities played out on her property. Maybe she confronted Max about it. Would he have killed her if she did? Maybe his visit to my bookstore, incriminating his relatives, was really just a way to deflect suspicion. Was it possible Adelaide's death had nothing to do with the spell book?

Max shook his head, his eyes welling. "No. Gram was supportive. Well, maybe she didn't like the hacking, but I never did anything bad."

I walked over to the far wall, perusing the contents of a shelf. It was mostly computer equipment, technical manuals, and few old, broken china teacups. "Where are your grandmother's things? My neighbor said she had this place fixed up nice, but all I see is computer equipment and broken stuff."

Max's eyes dropped to the floor. "She did have it set up nice, but the past few years—after she got sick—she didn't come out here so much. That's when she said I could use it. She hadn't really used it in a long time anyway, and most of the stuff was from the big house that she was storing here. We moved most of it over to the historical society."

My eyes narrowed. "Moved it, or sold it to Felicity Bates?"

Max screwed up his face. "Felicity Bates? No, she's awful. I wouldn't sell her anything."

"That's not how your stepmother feels. She seems to be acquiring quite a collection for Felicity."

"That figures. I have a trust fund. I don't need to sell things. And I sure as hell wouldn't sell off family heirlooms. Gram always said to make sure it all stays in the family. I'd tell my dad, but he won't stand up to Lisa."

I crossed to the empty window seat, which was surrounded by built-in shelves. The shelves were empty. "And what about your grandmother's books? Where are they?"

Max nodded at a brown water stain on the ceiling above the shelves. "Most of them got ruined. The ones that could be salvaged, I packed away and brought to the society."

My stomach tightened. What if the spell book had been ruined? Would that be good or bad? If it had been thrown out or destroyed, that meant that Felicity, or anyone who wanted to use it for evil intent, couldn't get their hands on it. But did that also mean that Adelaide would haunt me forever about it?

I continued my perusal of the room while Striker questioned Max about the morning Adelaide was found. He was also perusing the room as he talked. I was looking for the book, but what was Striker looking for? Evidence for Adelaide's murder case? It seemed unlikely any would be in the cottage if she was killed in her bed. Maybe he thought Max had brought it here to hide it. I glanced out the window at the spot where I'd seen the earth disturbed the first night I'd been here. Had Max buried evidence there?

I spun from the window, only to bump into Striker. He'd made his way around the room but apparently didn't find what he'd been looking for. Maybe I should tell him about the disturbed earth in the daisy field.

"I didn't have anything to do with my grandmother's death, if that's what you guys are looking for. I told you, Aunt Josie lied about being there that morning, so why aren't you interrogating her?" Max asked.

"What do you mean she lied?" Striker asked.

Max shot me a look. "You really didn't tell him?"

"No."

"Tell me what?" Striker frowned at me. I was in trouble.

"My surveillance camera caught Aunt Josie leaving the house early that morning. Before Gram was ... discovered." Max choked out the last word then continued. "Later on she claimed she'd been in the house, asleep in the library, the whole time. Why would she lie if she wasn't guilty?"

"Good question," Striker answered Max but was staring at me. "It would have been nice to know that before."

My cheeks flamed. I probably should have told him, but I'd promised Max, and I didn't like to go back on my word. "Sorry."

Max sat down at the leather office chair in front of the monitors, and his fingers tapped on the keys, bringing the monitors to life. "Well, if you guys are done, I'd like to get back to my game. I bet my buddy that I could make it past the dungeon and into level five tonight."

"We're done." Striker grabbed my elbow and propelled me toward the door. "If you think of anything else that might be of interest, let me know."

"Just what were you looking for in there?" Striker asked once we were outside.

"What were you?"

"Evidence."

"Did you see any?"

"No, but if I'd known about Josie, maybe I would have gone over there first." Striker jerked his head toward the Hamilton house as he dragged me away from the cottage. "You do realize that not telling me about that could be considered obstruction of justice. Maybe even aiding and abetting a criminal."

"Sorry, Max made me promise." I glanced at the daisy field as he pulled me past. "But there is something I can tell you that might help."

"What?"

"When I was here the other night, Pandora was digging in one spot...and it looked to me like that spot had been disturbed before."

Striker stopped short, his gaze swinging to the daisy field. "Where?"

I led him over to the spot. It was hard to tell what was from Pandora digging and what had been there before. Since it had been a few days, the daisies had sprung back up. "It was here. The flowers were all trampled."

Striker took out his flashlight and aimed it on the spot. He scuffed some of the dirt with the toe of his boot. "It's hard to tell when this happened." He glanced back at the cottage. "Do you think Max knows something's buried out here? He did come out and warn you off when he saw you here."

"I'm not sure. He said there was a time capsule, but that's hardly anything to worry about. He seems like a nice kid, and Adelaide ..."

"What about Adelaide?"

I had been about to say Adelaide had said he was a good kid, but I couldn't tell Striker that. "Umm... she let him use the cottage. It might not have been him that buried it, though. I thought I saw wheelchair tracks coming from the mansion."

Striker pursed his lips as he studied the ground. "I doubt the killer would bury something in this field. It's out in the open. If you were burying evidence that implicated you in a murder, would you bury it in an open field like this?"

He had a point. "I guess not. I wouldn't want to be seen, so I'd probably stick to the more secluded gardens near the house."

"It was probably just a dog that came out here and buried a bone," Striker suggested. "Pandora must've smelled it and wanted to dig it up."

I reluctantly let Striker lead me away. He was probably right.

"So what made you come here tonight, anyway?" Striker asked. "Are you following me?"

"*Me* following *you*?" I was pretty sure that *he* had been following *me*. "What are you talking about?"

"I saw you everywhere today. Passed you on the way into town. Saw you at the cafe. What gives?" He glanced down at me, his face softening. "Not that I don't like seeing you everywhere...or having you chase after me."

"I'm not chasing after you," I huffed. Images of the oversized glass of Pepper's togetherness tea that I'd guzzled down the night before came to mind. Was the tea bringing us together? Normally I'd be happy, but right now I needed time away from Striker, or I'd never be able to find the darn spell book.

Striker walked me to my Jeep, opened the door, and tucked me inside. He leaned down to talk to me through the open window.

"I'd love to stay and chat, but I'm on duty." A flicker of emotion softened his gray eyes. "It seems like we're ships passing in the night lately, but I'd like to remedy that."

My stomach did a flip-flop, and I looked into his sincere gray eyes. "Me too."

"Good. Then if you stop butting into my case, I can get it finished quickly, and we can schedule in some time...alone." He leaned in and dropped a soft kiss on my lips, then before I could say a word he turned and strode back to his sheriff car.

I felt a little disappointed that he hadn't made any more solid plans. Then again, it was probably for the best. Even if we managed to carve out some alone time, I was sure Adelaide's ghost would ruin it.

Chapter 18

The moon peeked out from behind a cloud, illuminating the ground around the Hamilton mansion. Pandora didn't need a full moon to see, nor did the dozens of cats who had volunteered for the mission and were now sitting in strategic spots around the house, with their extrasensory skills dialed up to the highest notch.

The cats surrounded the house, forming the shape of a pentagram. The shape amplified the cat's skills, giving them extreme sensitivity to items of magical powers. Alone, each cat was able to sense magic. Good and evil. But pinpointing a small item within a large space was only possible when they combined their efforts.

Pandora scrunched up her nose, concentrating on her abilities and homing in on the house, but it was no use. She didn't feel a thing.

"I'm not feeling it," said Dewey, as if reading her mind. Dewey's white chest glowed in the moonlight, the orange tips of his striped fur standing on end from the static electricity generated by the cats' paranormal efforts. Dewey was

formerly one of the feral cats of Mystic Notch who had found a forever home and had volunteered to help on this important mission.

"Me either," Pandora said and turned to the cat on the other side of her, an older but very wise Siamese named Thunder. "What about you?"

"Not a thing."

Inkspot appeared beside her. "It seems as if the book is no longer in the house...if it ever was there."

"I know. Maybe Willa was wrong. At least now I can discourage her from coming here..." Something at the edge of the field caught Pandora's eye. A splash of light illuminated the daisy field in front of the stone cottage. A familiar scent drifted over to her. The scent of her human. Willa and Striker were looking at the area she'd dug in the other night. She'd sensed something there, but her senses had not been dialed up, and she'd not had the benefit of other cat companions, so she wasn't sure if it was something as important as a spell book.

"Isn't that your human?" Inkspot asked.

"Yes. I dug there the other night. There is something there ... but I couldn't be sure what. Perhaps it is the book."

"We should check it out after the humans have —"

"Stop that! You're stealing Hamilton family heirlooms!" a woman's voice blared from the house.

"I'm not stealing. This stuff is as much mine as it is yours." A second woman's voice. "Tell her, David!"

"Well, technically Mom's will never said anything about the household items—" The man's voice was so soft that Pandora had to angle her ears forward to pick up the words.

"Oh sure, you won't say boo to anyone in your family, even your weirdo son. What's he doing out in the cottage, anyway? Probably watching porn."

"My nephew is not watching porn."

"How would you know, Josie? You can't even keep track of your own daughters. Why, one of them is upstairs with that boyfriend of hers doing God knows what right now."

"We weren't doing anything up there!" a young girl's voice cut in.

"That's right. My girls are good girls."

"Good girls?" The original woman snorted. "Why, look at the way this one dresses. She looks like Elvira. And anyway, how would you know? You're usually three sheets to the wind."

"I am not three sheetsh to the wind." The words were slightly slurred.

"What's that in your hand? Is that great-great-great-grandma Hamilton's flow blue soup tureen? That came over on the Mayflower!" A different young female voice this time.

"Put that stuff down. How many times do I have to tell you not to be selling off the family goods?" This time a crotchety-sounding old lady.

"You're not the boss of me," the accused stealer said. *"And who are you to say, anyway? You aren't even part of the Hamilton family, Marion."*

"Why, I never!"

Pandora worried that the old woman, whom she now realized was Adelaide's wheelchair-bound twin sister, was going to have a coronary, by the shrill sound of her voice.

"Shhh... Auntie Marion. Don't listen to her. Come outside. The cool night will calm you."

The door on the side of the house opened, and a dark-haired girl rolled Marion out onto the stone patio. From everything Pandora had heard, she assumed that girl was Adelaide's granddaughter Evie. The argument continued inside, but Pandora zoned them out and focused on the two women on the patio.

"Now calm down, Aunty. It's not good to get too excited at your age."

"Did you see her? She'll rob us blind!"

"No, she won't. We'll stop her. Now take a deep breath and look up at the beautiful moon. That will calm you down."

"You and your moon. It doesn't have any powers, you know."

"I think it's very soothing. Do you want me to wheel you around the grounds or through the fields like the other day?"

"No! I can wheel myself around quite nicely, thank you very much."

Evie wrestled a flyaway hair into place, only to have it zing out again. Pandora's own hairs were still feeling the effects of the static electricity, though that was waning now, as most of the cats had dialed down their senses.

"Okay then, we'll just sit out here and ..." Evie's voice broke off, and she turned in Pandora's direction, craning her neck and squinting her eyes. Pandora shuddered. It was almost as if the girl could see right into her.

"Do you see something out there?" Evie asked.

"What? No, there's nothing out there, silly girl."

"It sounds like there is much unrest among the humans." Otis had come up to join them. His words drew Pandora's attention from the two women.

"Yes. But that is none of our affair," Inkspot said. "We have done what we came to do. The spell book is not in that house."

Otis turned a concerned eye toward the Hamilton mansion, his gaze drifting over the two women on the patio to the lighted windows of the house. "The spell book is not, but somebody evil is."

"That's hardly news. We know we need to watch out for one of them." Inkspot turned his head toward the stone cottage. "Pandora's human is gone now. We can go see what is so important in the field."

Most of the other cats had dispersed, their mission complete. Even though they had not located the book of spells, at least they knew one place where it was not. Pandora led Inkspot, Otis, and a few of the others from Elspeth's barn to the spot in the daisy field. Though it was dark, they could clearly see the marks where she had dug the night before.

Pandora sniffed the earth, the sour smell of fear curling her whiskers. "There is something in here, but I don't think it's the book."

Otis's whiskers twitched, his nose pointing in the air. "There is much here. I smell hopes and dreams, memories and aspirations, fear and death." He looked around at them dramatically. "But no magic."

Pandora sniffed again. She hadn't smelled all that. But Otis had been periodically exhibiting extraordinary powers ever since he drank a magic extract that nearly killed him. She assumed it had affected his power of smell.

The other cats took turns checking the area out, some of them putting their noses close to the ground, others scenting the air. They all agreed something was buried there, but it was not the book of spells.

Sasha turned in a slow circle, sniffing the air. "The good news is that I don't smell Fluff. He must not be onto this place."

"Well, since the spell book isn't here, that's no surprise. Maybe he was smarter than us and knew not to come here."

"Smarter?" Kelley scoffed. "I don't think so."

"Now what?" Snowball, her white fur gleaming silver in the moonlight, asked. "How will we get the spell book to Elspeth?"

"We have to figure out where it is, or depend on the humans to do it," Inkspot said. "Either way, it better happen soon. I sense that time is not on our side."

Chapter 19

The next day I went to the Hamilton house again on the pretext of having lost something when I was visiting the day before. John, the butler, had actually given me the idea when I'd visited with Pepper. I knew it was kind of lame, but I had to get back into that library. The cottage had been a bust, and the library was my only lead.

I stood at the door, mustering my courage to knock, when a car pulled into the driveway behind me.

I turned to look, my stomach plummeting at the sight of the brown Crown Victoria sheriff car. Striker!

I tried not to wilt under his glare as he exited the car and mounted the steps. "What are you doing here?"

"I left something here the other day."

Striker's brow creased into a "V" of suspicion. "What?"

"A bracelet my grandmother—"

I was saved from elaborating on the lie by the door opening. For once I was glad to see the annoying butler, whose skeptical eyes darted from me to Striker. At least Striker, in his brown sheriff uniform, looked as if he was there on official business. "Is there a problem?"

John's eyes flicked back to me when he said "problem," as if he associated the very word with me.

"I'd like to talk to Josie Hamilton, if I may," Striker said.

John hesitated then opened the door, inviting Striker in. I slipped in behind him, hoping I could just tag along and eavesdrop on Striker's conversation. I assumed he was there to question Josie about Max's surveillance footage of her leaving the house the morning of Adelaide's death.

John led us to the sitting room and excused himself to summon Josie.

"What are you still doing here?" Striker hissed.

"Looking for my bracelet." I grappled under the cushion for the fictional bracelet. "I think I lost it when I was here the other day."

Striker slid skeptical eyes in my direction. "What bracelet? I don't know how you knew I would be coming here now, but I think you're just trying to spy—"

"You wanted to speak to me?" Josie interrupted as she entered the room.

"Just a few questions," Striker said.

"Whatever for?" Josie's voice wobbled nervously. "Is it one of my girls? Julie's boyfriend, Brian?"

"No, none of that. I just have some questions about the morning your mother died."

"Oh." The air whooshed out of her, and she collapsed in a chair. "It was so awful. I loved my mother deeply."

Striker's brow ticked up. "Of course. And where were you that morning?"

Her eyes snapped over to him. "What do you mean, where was I? I was here in the house. I live here."

"So you were in the house when it was discovered that your mother had passed?"

Josie looked down, picking at the hem of her off-white linen shirt. "Yes."

"Another family member mentioned you weren't in your room."

Josie looked up, her eyes narrowing. "That's right. I was in the library. I'd fallen asleep in there."

"Are you sure?"

"Of course I'm sure! Why are you asking all these questions anyway? Wait a minute. Are you implying there was something suspicious about my mother's death?" Josie shook her head. "No.

Mom had cancer. She died in her sleep...she looked very peaceful."

"How do you know that? Your family said you didn't show up until after the ambulance came."

This was getting interesting. I didn't dare move—I didn't want to interrupt the line of questioning or for Striker to ease up so that I wouldn't overhear.

"Just why are you asking this?" Josie repeated.

"We have reason to believe there may have been some foul play. I'm just checking all the angles."

Josie's eyes welled. She fiddled with the bottom of her shirt some more. "And you think I know something about it?"

"Well, ma'am, I have conflicting testimony. You say you were there, but your family members say you didn't come until the ambulance was almost leaving. You could see how that might look a little funny, can't you?"

First she looked indignant, then uncertain, then her face crumbled, and she sobbed into her hands. "You don't understand. It's so hard..."

"Understand what, ma'am?" Striker remained impassive.

My head ping-ponged between Striker and Josie. Maybe she would confess and then tell us where the book was.

She sniffed a loud, wet sniff and plucked a tissue out of the holder beside her chair. "I wasn't really lying. I was here...well, for most of the time."

"Okay, tell me what happened." Striker used his most persuasive voice.

"I looked in on my mother, and she looked uncomfortable. I had forgotten to fill a prescription the day before ... so I ran out to the pharmacy. When I came back, she was... well, the EMTs were here." She dissolved into a round of sobbing.

I remembered Gus's phone call where the medical examiner had said they found opiates in Adelaide's blood. If she was doped up that much, how could she have been uncomfortable? Wouldn't Josie have noticed her mother was drugged up? And if Josie had forgotten to fill the prescription, where did the drugs in her system come from?

"Why did you lie about where you were?" Striker asked.

She waved her hands in the air and hiccuped. "The family is so nosy, always wanting to know everything. I didn't think it was any of their business. I didn't want them getting on me because I forgot to fill the darn prescription."

"So when you looked in on your mother, she was still alive?"

"Yes," she whispered, her gaze dropping to the floor.

"Are you sure?"

"What are you trying to imply?"

"Well, it just seems odd that you would look in on her and then leave, and not an hour later she's found dead."

"Are you trying to say I had something to do with it? She was an old woman. She was ill. I don't see why you think someone killed her."

"Did you notice anything unusual about her? Did you see anyone coming or going to her room that morning?"

Josie chewed her bottom lip. Trying to remember, or making up a lie? "I didn't notice anything unusual. She was so still in the bed. I didn't see anyone near her room."

"Can anyone corroborate your story? Someone who might have seen you, maybe someone in one of the bedrooms near yours or your mother's?"

"Only Evie and Julie are in my wing. They were asleep."

"You didn't see either of them?"

"No."

"What time were you in her room?" Striker asked.

"I think it was around seven-thirty. I wasn't exactly looking at my watch."

"Is it part of your normal routine, then, to check on her that early?"

"No, actually, I usually get up much later, but something out in the hallway woke me."

"Something?"

"A noise. Squeaking."

"So someone else was out there?"

Josie shrugged. "I guess so. I figured it might be the butler lurking around or using the dumbwaiter to bring up linens. That old thing is across from my room, and it makes a lot of noises."

"But you didn't see him or anyone else?"

She shook her head.

"According to the police report, your mother's room is at the north end of the hall from yours. Your two daughters are at the south end. Are there stairs at either end for access?"

"No. Mom's suite is at the very end. The only way to get to it is to walk past the girls' room then mine since the only entry point is the south end of the hall, where the main stairway is located."

"So your daughters might have seen something. Would either of them be up at that time?"

Josie shook her head. "No. They sleep in. If you are implying one of them had something to do with this..."

Striker held up his hand. "Not at all. Just trying to find someone to verify your whereabouts."

"Verify her whereabouts? Someone needs to, because she usually can't." Lisa glared at me from the doorway, then her eyes settled on Striker. She straightened, and a predatory smile bloomed on her face. "Well, hello there."

I didn't like the way she sashayed into the room or the way she was looking at Striker, but I knew he was almost done questioning Josie, and I had better make my excuses to get into library quickly. Besides, if Lisa was kept busy in here, then I wouldn't worry about running into her trying to steal the family fortune in there.

"Excuse me." All eyes swiveled in my direction. "May I use the bathroom?"

Striker shot me a look, but I plastered a benign smile on my face and ignored him.

"Certainly," Josie said. "It's in the hall and to the left."

I practically jumped off the sofa and hurried into the hall. I peeked into the library, grateful that the room was empty. I slipped inside and pushed the door almost shut, enough so no one walking by could glance in and see me but so that I could also hear if someone came down the hall.

I went right to the painting. I'd already looked at most of the books in the shelves underneath, and a glance at the rest didn't yield anything titled *Betty's Recipes*. What about the painting itself—

could there be a safe or hiding spot behind it? I grabbed the edges, thinking to lift it off the wall, but the darn thing weighed a ton. I tugged, but it wouldn't budge. Was it glued to the wall?

I tilted my head to look at the bottom. Slipping my fingers underneath, I pushed it out from the wall just to see if there was a safe or niche in the wall behind it. There was no safe or niche. I let the painting thud back against the wall with a sigh, and that was when I saw it. The nameplate on the bottom. Daisy Edgars-Hamilton.

Just as Adelaide had implied, she hadn't been referring to the daisy *flower*, she'd been referring to her ancestor—Daisy.

"What are you doing?"

Striker was standing in the doorway, his arms crossed over his chest.

"What? Oh. Nothing." I couldn't tell him about Daisy, because if I did I'd have to tell him about the spell book and Adelaide's ghost. I didn't want to hold out on information that might help his investigation, but nothing I'd discovered provided additional clues into Adelaide's murder.

"That seems like a funny place to look for your bracelet," he said.

"What bracelet?"

"Just as I thought." He grabbed me by the hand and pulled me from the room. "You're up to something, aren't you?"

"Me? No." He propelled me toward the front door, nodding to John as the butler opened it for us.

We stepped onto the granite steps, and the door shut.

"What did you find out?" Striker asked me.

"Nothing. I'd seen Lisa in the library before and thought maybe there might be a clue in there." Technically, that wasn't a lie. "What did you find out? Do you know why someone would have killed Adelaide? You don't think it was Josie, her own daughter, do you?"

"I'm not sure if Josie is the killer." Striker glanced back at the house. "But I am sure about one thing. Josie Hamilton was lying about something."

Chapter 20

Pandora greeted me at the bookstore with a stilted meow. I tried to appease her with some catnip before getting to work on cataloging more books. I entered a stack of books in my inventory system, printed off labels for them, and proceeded to put them away in their various sections. The mindless job left me room to think about Josie.

What had she been lying about? Her story about rushing out to the pharmacy didn't sit well. Could she have been the one that killed Adelaide? There was one way to rule her out...if I knew Adelaide's time of death and the pharmacy had a record of the transaction, then that would prove she was not in the house when Adelaide died.

Gus would never tell me the time of death, but I knew someone who would—her deputy Jimmy. Jimmy owed me. I got my phone from the front desk and punched in his number.

"What do you want this time, Willa?" Jimmy answered the phone, apparently on to me.

"Hey, I don't always call because I want something." *Did I?*

"Well, it has been a while," Jimmy said. "How's Pandora? Scooter is getting along at my place just fine."

Scooter was a little feral tuxedo cat Jimmy had adopted. I gazed out the window as he launched into a monologue about the cat and what was going on in his life. I mechanically grunted out various appropriate noises as I waited for an opening to ask about Adelaide's time of death.

Across the street, I saw the flaming-red locks of Felicity Bates. She had her white long-haired cat on a leash. Odd, because I thought Felicity hated cats. I watched as the cat wound itself around her ankles, rubbing its cheek against her red stilettos. Pandora was watching too, the hairs on her back standing on end.

Felicity was arguing with someone. No surprise there. I adjusted my angle and craned my neck to see who it was. That *was* a surprise—it was Marion and Evie. Marion was seated in her wheelchair, waving her fist in Felicity's face. Evie, who stood behind the chair, was bent toward Marion, apparently soothing her. I wondered what that was about. Maybe Marion was having it out with Felicity over trying to buy the Hamilton family treasures.

"So how's things going with you?" Jimmy's voice in my ear brought my thoughts back to the reason for my call.

"Just great. Book sales are up. Pandora is in rare form. You know my grandmother was a good friend of Adelaide Hamilton's, don't you?"

"Yeah." Jimmy drew out the end of the word, his voice wary.

"Well, I'm trying to do something for my grandma. Something she asked for in her will."

"And that has something to do with Adelaide?"

"Yes, and it would be really helpful to know her time of death."

"Huh? Why the heck would you need to know that?"

"Umm ... well, I can't really say, but if you could tell me, I'd owe you one."

Silence. I checked my phone to make sure we were still connected.

Finally I heard a loud sigh, and Jimmy said, "Well, I suppose it won't hurt to tell you that. It's not like we're keeping it a secret. Adelaide died between six and seven a.m."

I glanced over at the pharmacy across the street, double-checking the hours on the sign on the door. Icy fingers danced up my spine.

If what Jimmy had just said was true, then Adelaide was already dead when Josie claimed to have looked in on her.

***

Now things were getting confusing. Had Josie killed Adelaide for the spell book? Or had she just failed to notice that her mother was dead when she looked in on her? She did seem kind of out of it, but I had assumed her state was due to her grief over her mother's death. I didn't know what Josie was like before that, though.

Josie had mentioned that a noise in the hall had woken her. Evie's room was down the hall. Evie had been seen out in the fields, worshipping the moon. Someone like that might be after a spell book.

The motive for Adelaide's murder might not have been the spell book at all. But what? Money? I doubted I could find out what was in the will, but if the motive had been greed, then Lisa was at the top of my suspect list. But why wouldn't she just wait it out instead of risk going to jail for murder? Adelaide didn't have many more years, and it appeared as if Lisa lived a cushy lifestyle as it is. The only reason would be if Adelaide was going to change her will and cut Lisa out somehow, or if Lisa wanted out of the marriage and that would mean she would inherit nothing.

As I closed up the shop that night, I circled back to my earlier thought about Josie killing Adelaide for the spell book. If Josie was after the book, the only reason she'd have to kill Adelaide would be because Adelaide was protecting it—keeping her from it—somehow. If Adelaide had given up the location, Josie would have it by now, but if her clues were as cryptic as the ones she'd given me, Josie would still be looking. *If* in fact she'd been the killer *and* the book was the reason.

I had a gut feeling that *Betty's Recipes* had not yet been found, and if Josie was searching, then maybe my best bet was to follow her.

Adelaide didn't pop in to persuade me otherwise, so I went home for dinner then put on my all-black outfit and headed out. Pandora would not take no for an answer, and I soon found myself skulking across the field toward the Hamilton estate with her leading the way as if she knew exactly where she was going.

We hunkered down in an area of tall grass. The grass was trampled as if someone had been there before, scoping out the house. Or maybe it was wild animals. I looked around nervously—there were a variety of animals out here. Coyote, bobcats, deer, black bears. I hoped this wasn't one of their favorite spots.

Pandora focused her golden-green eyes on the Hamilton house, her whiskers twitching in the humid night air. Yellow light glowed in the windows. I could see people moving around, and once in a while a word or two drifted across the field, muted by the sounds of frogs peeping. Pandora stood, her tail sticking straight in the air—the kink at the end pointing toward the mansion—seconds before an obscure door at the side of the house opened and Josie stepped out.

She wore a long, thin sweater over a tank top and jeans. I watched as she hurried to a white rose bush that trailed up a white lattice archway. She inspected a few of the flowers then took a pair of scissors from her pocket and cut one off.

Pandora was way ahead of me, already trotting to the edge of the field by the time Josie turned and disappeared behind the back of the house. Where was she going? I rose from my crouched position and jogged in that direction, sticking to the field, away from the manicured lawns of the house.

Josie was on the other side of the mansion now, walking toward the woods. How odd. The behavior seemed like something I would expect from Evie. My gaze drifted past Josie to the woods, and I remembered what I'd seen there the other day. The Hamilton family cemetery. Was Josie paying respects to one of her ancestors? Not Adelaide, though. Family cemeteries on private land hadn't been used for burial in over fifty years. But maybe her grandmother or another ancestor ... like Daisy Hamilton. It was likely Daisy was buried the cemetery or her remains were in the mausoleum. Adelaide had mentioned the book was "with Daisy" or something like that. If it was in there, I had to get to that mausoleum and stop Josie from finding it!

As if reading my thoughts, Pandora was already trotting across the yard toward the woods. I followed, sticking to the shadows and unlit parts of the yard.

The mausoleum was a gray cement building with no windows and a wrought-iron door. I peered into the door, my eyes barely able to see the figure of Josie inside, standing over a cement vault. She dropped the rose on top, patted the edge, and turned toward the door. I jerked back by instinct, flattening myself against the outside. Josie didn't see me. She exited and headed toward the house without a backward glance. Did she have the book? It didn't look like it—her hands were empty.

She hadn't been in there long enough to search for anything, so what had she been doing?

A ball of fear tightened in my stomach as I eyed the dark opening. I had to go in and check things out for myself. Hopefully I wouldn't be swarmed by ghosts who all wanted something from me.

The inside of the mausoleum was cloaked in the damp smell of wet earth and decaying leaves. The air was stagnant, and Pandora let out a little "Mew", her whiskers twitching violently.

The only light came from the moonbeams spilling in from the open iron door and a lone flickering candle that cast eerie shadows on the walls. There were three casket-sized tombs, the edges of their concrete tops decorated with scrolled designs. The far wall had several niches with names engraved on stones. Cremation ashes?

I crossed to the tomb where Josie had been standing. On top lay two white roses. Two? Josie had only brought one. And why? The inscription on the top yielded a clue. The ancestor inside—Rose Chester Hamilton—had died on this very day one hundred years ago. Did Josie bring it as a remembrance to a long-dead ancestor she'd never known?

Dang! This whole thing probably had nothing to do with the spell book...

"*Meow!*" Pandora scratched at the vault on the other end as if she were trying to tell me something. Crazy? Not any more than everything else that was happening. I bent down to look at the area she was pawing, the name causing a jolt of adrenaline—Daisy Edgars-Hamilton.

Had Adelaide hidden the book inside Daisy's vault? Weren't these things sealed?

I pushed on the top just in case. The scratchy sound of concrete grating against concrete answered the question as to whether or not they were sealed. I pushed harder, not sure that I actually wanted to look inside but knowing that I had to. Now would be a great time for Adelaide to pop up and give me some guidance.

"What are you doing?"

My heart leaped into my throat. I whirled around to see Striker standing in the doorway.

"Please tell me you haven't turned to grave robbing."

"Very funny. Come help me push. I need to see what's inside here."

"Inside? Probably a dead person. What are you looking for?"

Good question. I couldn't tell him about the spell book, but I didn't want to lie outright, so I fudged it. "I saw Josie come out here and thought maybe she was hiding evidence."

"In there?" Striker frowned at the vault. "And how did you see Josie? Are you spying on her?"

"How did you see me? Are you spying on me?"

"I had a funny feeling you would do something stupid tonight. Turns out I was right." Striker sounded frustrated—I assumed with me—but he stepped closer and pushed on the cover.

The top slid a couple of inches. Striker pulled out his flashlight and aimed it inside. I took a deep breath and looked in, expecting to see the top of an old casket. Apparently they didn't use caskets one hundred years ago in the mausoleum, because inside were the remnants of a tattered dress, ivory-white bones, a skull looking up at me in a silent scream. No book.

"So much for hiding it with favorite relatives," Striker muttered.

"Huh?" Had he said something? I was still reeling from looking at the decayed corpse and didn't quite catch what it was.

"I don't see any evidence in there, do you?" he said.

"Oh. No," I said. "Maybe we should check the other—"

Voices outside cut off my words. "Shhh." I grabbed Striker and pulled him into the shadows. The voices grew closer.

"Are you following me?" a young woman hissed.

"No. What are you doing out here with that flower, anyway?" A young man.

"Leaving a white rose for my great-great-grandmother. It's her death day, and it's a family tradition. Not that you need to know about family traditions, because if I have my way about it, you won't be hanging around my sister for very long."

That explained the white roses and what Josie was doing out here. It also explained Evie's nighttime trip, but what was Brian doing out here? Looking for the book, or maybe making sure Evie didn't get her hands on it?

Brian laughed. "Well, luckily you don't have any say in who Julie dates. You don't have her under your spell anymore, Evie."

"We'll see about that. I'm not going to stand by and let you ..."

"*Hiss!*" Pandora stood at the door, her back arched, hairs on end.

"Hey!" A white rose fell to the ground just outside the doorway.

"*Meow!*" Pandora let out a loud wail.

"What are you doing in here, Kitty?" Evie swooped down, trying to grab Pandora, who jumped out of the way, hissing and spitting. "Come here, Kitt—"

She glanced up, stopping mid-sentence, her eyes narrowed as she scanned the interior of the mausoleum. I shrank back against the wall, but it was no use. She homed in on Striker and me, her forehead creasing as she picked up the fallen rose and stood. "Just what are *you* doing in here? Aren't you the people who were accusing my mom yesterday?"

"We weren't accusing, just asking," Striker said.

Evie stuck her hands on her hips. "I don't think I like you poking into Hamilton family business."

"I'm the sheriff. It's my job to poke."

Evie turned to Willa. "And what's your excuse?"

"My gram was friends with your gram." I shrugged, hoping that would be enough of an excuse.

Evie's face softened. "She was?"

I nodded.

Evie walked slowly to the vault and laid the rose on top. In the dark light with the lone candle flickering, her pale skin and dark hair made her look eerily like some sort of vampire or witch. I moved closer to Striker.

"My mom didn't kill my gram. There's more to this than meets the eye. Forces at work you two wouldn't understand." Evie turned toward the door. "Where is that cat?"

Where *was* the cat? I looked around the small room, but she was nowhere to be seen. I reminded myself not to worry—Pandora could take care of herself.

Striker wasn't worried either. He'd reverted to sheriff mode. "Did you see anyone near your grandmother's room the morning she died?"

"No, I was asleep. I heard Aunt Marion's wheelchair, and then I heard her screaming."

"Was anyone acting odd, or did you see anything unusual?" Striker asked.

Evie snorted. "The whole family acts odd, but if you ask me, Julie's boyfriend, Brian, is up to something." Evie jerked her head toward the door, and I realized Brian wasn't out there. He must have taken off when Evie came in.

"Why do you say that?" I asked.

Evie's face turned rueful. "I can tell he doesn't really like Julie. He's after something, but I can't convince her of that. That's okay. I have other ways to show everyone what he's really made of."

"Do you have any proof that he's up to something?" Striker asked.

"No, just a feeling," Evie said. "You still didn't explain what you are doing in my family mausoleum."

I expected Striker to say something official, but when he didn't, I came up with the first thing I could think of. "Chasing after my cat. She ran in here."

Evie made a face. "What was your cat doing in my yard?"

"Umm... she got away."

"Right." Evie looked at me skeptically. "I'm not sure what you are up to, but you better tread carefully." She turned to Striker. "And unless you have a warrant, I think you need to get off the property."

She stood back and pointed to the door. I didn't mind leaving. I'd already seen what I came to see. Striker and I exchanged a shrug then headed out. As we walked across the field back to our cars, Pandora darted out of nowhere and fell into step beside us.

I had mixed feelings about our visit. I hadn't found the book, but I'd learned something more about the Hamilton family. Evie suspected Brian was up to something, but she had ulterior motives, which made me wonder...was he really up to something, or was she just telling us that to use him as a scapegoat to cover up her own involvement?

Chapter 21

Striker's police car was parked behind my Jeep on the dirt road. I was hoping to escape without him asking any more questions, so I quick-stepped it to the Jeep and hauled open the driver's door. Pandora prevented me from hopping in right away by scooting in herself, and by then Striker had caught up. He put his hand on my arm and held me back.

"Not so fast." He pulled me gently from the door and shut it. "What were you really doing in there?"

"I told you. I followed Josie in there and thought she might be hiding evidence."

"Really? Then how come you were trying to pry open the vault on one side when Josie had clearly been at the other vault with the white roses on it?"

"I was going to pry all of them open. I didn't know which one she would have stashed the evidence in."

A white mist appeared to the left of Striker, and I had to struggle not to sigh and roll my eyes. It figured that Adelaide would show up now.

Luckily Striker appeared to be deep in thought, his gaze looking off at something behind me.

"Honestly, Willa, I heard you were good at this sort of thing, but you couldn't prove that to me. You haven't found the book yet," Adelaide said.

I waved my hand for her to go away, but instead of Adelaide disappearing, my gesture caught Striker's attention. "What are you doing?"

"Mosquito."

To my amazement, Striker's eyes drifted to follow something over my shoulder, almost as if he actually saw a mosquito.

"It's not in the mausoleum. How the hell would I put a book in there, anyway?" Adelaide rolled her eyes. "Do you think I could open one of those vaults?"

This was frustrating. I really wanted to talk to Adelaide and see if she could give me something more specific about the spell book, but I had to get rid of Striker first. He looked as if he was frustrated too. Probably at me. Maybe if I turned the tide and started interrogating *him,* he'd get mad and drive away, and I could talk to Adelaide in peace.

"What were *you* doing in the mausoleum, and don't give me that lame excuse that you were following me around." I narrowed my eyes at him. "I bet you think there's evidence in there, don't you?"

"Evidence? Yes, there could be." I was surprised he admitted that, but I wasn't sure he even realized what he'd said. He seemed distracted. Looking directly past me, he gritted his teeth and said, "But I didn't find anything."

"Of course you didn't find anything. The book isn't in there." Adelaide shook her head at Striker then turned back to me. "I don't know why you picked this young man. He seems to be quite daft."

Striker wasn't going anywhere. I had to think of another way to communicate with Adelaide. Maybe I could word things in such a way that she would know what I was talking about and wouldn't sound totally weird to Striker.

"If you could tell me exactly where it was, we could have this solved pretty quickly," I said, raising my brows at Adelaide.

"I told you. It's with Daisy." She tapped her index finger on her lips. "Now if I could only remember where I put that painting."

"It's in the library!" I blurted out.

"There's evidence in the library?" Striker asked.

"No. Did I say that? Well, there might be something in there." Shoot, I was really screwing up.

"Not *that* painting," Adelaide said. "The one in her blue satin gown..." Adelaide's voice trailed off, and she looked off in the distance, past Striker's shoulder. "Oh, Willa, please help me. I feel my Louis is slipping away."

" ...if I knew where." Striker was saying. I hadn't been paying attention to him, but I assumed he said he'd get the evidence if he knew where it was.

"Yeah, if only we knew where the evidence was, this mess would all be over and we could go back to normal," I agreed.

Striker frowned, his eyes tracking something that moved from his left to behind me. The mosquito? He shook his head. What was wrong with him?

"Louis is getting even closer. I can feel him near. You have to hurry, Willa!" Adelaide sounded desperate. If only she knew how badly I wanted to find that stupid book and have this all over with.

Striker grabbed my shoulders and moved me to the side with my back up against the Jeep. "This is ruining our relationship."

"You're telling me." I glared at Adelaide.

"Maybe when this is all over, we can finally be alone to pick up where we left off." Striker stepped closer. His left palm on the roof of my Jeep, his right cupping my chin, his thumb tracing my cheek. "Or maybe we could start now."

He leaned in, brushing his lips against mine. My eyes fluttered closed then flew open as I felt the cold, clammy mist of a ghost. Was Adelaide watching us? Creepy. She stood just behind Striker, a smile across her lips, and she gave a curt nod and then disappeared.

At least she had the decency to leave us to our private moment. Unfortunately, Adelaide had been as vague as usual. But I had gotten one concrete clue. Now I knew she'd hidden the book in a painting of Daisy. Not the one in the library, but another one. All I had to do was locate it. The logical place for a painting of a Hamilton family ancestor was inside the Hamilton mansion. I just hoped I hadn't already worn out my welcome.

***

Pandora thumped her tail on the front seat of the car as she watched Willa and Striker trying to ignore the ghosts of Adelaide and Louis swirling around them. She would have found the way they were trying to ignore their respective persistent ghosts amusing if she weren't in such a hurry to get back to Willa's so she could sneak over to Elspeth's barn and tell the cats of this new development.

While she waited, she mulled over the new clue. She now knew where the book was. Inside the painting of Daisy Hamilton in the blue dress. But where was the painting? It wasn't in the Hamilton house, nor was it buried in the yard in front of the cottage. She was sure of this because if the book were there, the cats' combined efforts the other night would have revealed its location.

She cast a tentative glance toward the cemetery. The mausoleum was empty now, but she had felt something evil there earlier, and now she had a pretty good idea who was trying to obtain the spell book. If Striker and Willa would just hurry up, she could bring this information to the cats and find out if one of them had any new information that would help them figure out where the book was.

She turned her attention back to the humans, scrunching down and using her telepathic skills to will them into breaking up their little tête-à-tête and leaving.

Louis was trying to communicate the same thing to Striker that Adelaide had just told Willa. The spell book could be in a painting. He didn't have the details of whose painting, but he knew Adelaide had hidden things in special compartments attached to the wooden stretchers in the back before. Too bad Louis had no idea where the painting was either. And it tugged at Pandora's heart that the two ghosts, Adelaide and Louis, could sense each other but were on different planes and could not connect, even though they were standing right next to each other!

By the way Willa and Striker were now mashing their lips together, Pandora could see they were having no trouble connecting. She was glad to see them together, but there were much more important things going on, so she amped up her telepathy in order for them to get a move on. She knew from past experience the two of them could keep up the lip mashing for quite some time, and there was no time for that now. Both Pandora and Willa had important work to do.

Chapter 22

The last time I'd gone to the Hamilton mansion, I'd been lucky enough to slip in along with Striker, so I hadn't used up my I-lost-something-here excuse. The excuse had seemed like a great idea at the time, but now that I was standing in front of the big oak door, waiting for someone to answer, I wasn't so sure. Maybe I should've taken Pandora's advice, as she seemed hell-bent on stopping me from coming to the Hamiltons', doing everything from coughing up a hairball to puncturing a hole in my shirt with her razor-sharp claws. But before I could turn and run, the door opened.

John, the butler, stood in the threshold, blocking my entrance. "You again."

I didn't let his sour attitude faze me. "Good morning. I seem to have lost something here on one of my previous visits. Do you think I could come in and look? I'm pretty sure it slipped off my wrist when I was sitting on the sofa. It's a bracelet that my grandmother gave me."

His brow wrinkled with skepticism. "Perhaps if you describe it, I will go look in the sofa for you."

"No, I'd really rather—"

"Who is it, John?" Josie's voice rang out from the hallway. John stepped back so she could see me, and her eyes widened.

"Oh dear. You better let her in." Josie nibbled her bottom lip as if my presence made her nervous. What was that about?

John pushed the door wide and jerked his head toward the hallway in an apparent invitation for me to enter, which I did quickly before Josie changed her mind.

"I lost my bracelet in the drawing room when I was here the other day," I explained to Josie, although she appeared to be more than willing to let me in anyway.

Josie frowned, and her gaze slid to John. "Right. Of course. Follow me."

I followed her down the hall slowly, my eyes flicking to each painting, my stomach sinking lower and lower as I realized none of them were of Daisy in the blue gown.

We came to the door of the sitting room, and I had no choice but to go in. Josie was already in there, waiting anxiously.

I headed over to the off-white linen sofa. "Sorry to intrude, but the bracelet was my grandmother's. The catch is loose, so it probably slipped off and fell behind the cushions..." I heard a scraping and clicking sound and turned around to see that Josie had pulled the pocket door shut, closing the room off from the hallway.

"I know why you're really here." She stared at me with dark, accusing eyes.

Nerves fluttered in my belly. Josie could be a killer, and by the way she was looking at me, she seemed to think I'd come for a reason other than to retrieve my bracelet. Had Evie told her about our run-in at the mausoleum? If she really did kill Adelaide for the spell book and thought I had discovered something, I could be in big trouble. Was that why Pandora seemed so intent on keeping me from coming here? I'd thought she was just mad that I wasn't bringing her. My gaze flicked nervously to the closed door. She could do anything, and no one would know.

"No, really, I was just looking for my—"

"Cut the crap." She walked toward me. "I know your boyfriend sent you."

"My boyfriend?"

"Yeah, that hunky sheriff. He sent you to get more information out of me, didn't he? He thinks a woman would seem more sympathetic. I know how you people work. You think I killed my own mother, don't you?"

I probably should have tried to persuade her that we thought no such thing. Probably should have lulled her into believing I was no threat and then bolted out of there, but my big mouth got me into trouble, and I blurted out: "Well, your story is a little suspicious, especially since we've verified with the ME that your mother was already dead at the time that you *say* you checked on her."

I was braced for her to attack me somehow, but to my surprise, Josie dissolved into tears and collapsed onto the nearest chair. "I know you think I did it, but I didn't. I swear."

I sat down on the sofa. Obviously there was more to Adelaide's death. I had to find out what Josie knew. "Okay. Why don't you tell me what happened, then."

She plucked a tissue out of a silver box on the table and dabbed at her red-rimmed eyes. "I didn't lie about what happened that morning. Well, not about *everything*. Most of it was the truth."

"Which part wasn't the truth?"

Josie sighed and looked down at the floor, her cheeks turning pink. "The part about her being alive."

"You knew she was dead when you looked in on her?"

"Yes, but I swear I thought she'd died in her sleep." Josie blew her nose loudly into the tissue.

"But why wouldn't you have said something? Why would you leave and go to the pharmacy and then lie about being in the library?"

She glanced back at the door as if making sure it was still closed and no one could hear us. "I knew once the pharmacy found out she was dead, her prescriptions would no longer be able to be filled."

"So you rushed out to the pharmacy to refill it before anyone found out. Why would you need to refill it, though, if she was dead?"

Josie hung her head in shame. "I'm not proud of this. I've been taking Mom's pills for quite some time. I was shocked when I found my mom, but I knew I couldn't help her. She was already gone." Her eyes took on a desperate, wild look. "I need those pills to get through the day. But you see this proves I had no motive to kill my mother. Quite the opposite, in fact. Her death has put me in a bad place because I can't get the prescription pills anymore."

I blew out a breath and sat back in the chair. That explained how she always seemed doped up or nervous. Either she was telling the truth, or she was a great actress. But if she was telling the truth, that meant she didn't kill Adelaide for the book. And if she didn't kill Adelaide, then who did?

Josie sobbed loudly into the tissue. "You do believe me? Don't you?"

I leaned forward and touched her arm. I did believe her. And not only that, since she seemed to be in a confessing mood, I figured it was a good time to earn her trust with sympathy so I could ask more questions. "I believe you, Josie."

Her shoulders relaxed. "Thank you. And you'll tell your boyfriend that it wasn't me? He won't arrest me, will he?"

"I'll make sure he doesn't arrest you," I assured her as if I had any control of what Striker would do. "Do you have any idea who would have wanted your mother dead?"

She shook her head and dabbed at her eyes with a fresh tissue. "I honestly thought she died in her sleep. But if someone really did kill her, then my money would be on that bitch Lisa."

"Lisa? Why?"

"To get her hands on my mother's money, of course."

"But why risk killing an old woman? It seems like Lisa has plenty of money. She wears nice clothes and has expensive jewelry. Seems like it wouldn't be worth the risk of getting caught, especially since she probably wouldn't have had to wait too long for your mother to die naturally."

Josie shrugged. "She's greedy. Wasn't satisfied with what she had. Always wanted more and more and more."

"Did you notice anything unusual about your mother that morning? Anything in her room that was out of place?"

"I'm not sure. It was such a shock. I did love my mother. Didn't want her to die. And she was lying there so still. I crept over to her to see if she was breathing. She wasn't. Her pillows were askew, and I adjusted them." She sucked in a breath and looked at me with wide eyes. "You don't think I ruined the evidence, do you? It's just that Mother always liked to have matching pillowcases, and one didn't match. So I put it on the bottom."

"I'm sure you didn't ruin anything." I didn't mention the part about how the pillow was likely askew because Adelaide was suffocated with it. "The police didn't process her room as a crime scene anyway because they didn't have probable cause until after the blood work came back."

"Oh, good."

I'd already asked about the recipe book on my first visit, and no one had admitted to knowing about it, so I decided to take a different route in my questioning. "Did your mom ever mention something important that she might have hidden away?"

"Important? Like diamonds or precious gems or silver? There was a silver tray that she—"

"Not like that. More like something she treasured but might not have a lot of monetary value."

"No, she just mentioned she didn't want Lisa stealing everything, so she was storing some of it in the cottage."

"The one that Max is using now?"

Josie nodded.

I gnawed on my bottom lip. I'd been in the cottage, and there were no family heirlooms. But would Adelaide have put the painting with the book in it there for safekeeping? Or would she have hidden it in plain sight?

"I noticed you have a lot of ancestral paintings in the hallway here. They're quite nice and probably worth a lot. Do you have a lot of them in the home?"

Josie snorted. "Those horrible old things? I should say not. Mother wouldn't let us take them down from the hall or the library, but we managed to get rid of the others, thankfully."

My heart lurched. Get *rid* of them? I hoped that after all this, she wasn't about to tell me they'd thrown the painting of Daisy in the blue gown in the dump or something. Surely Adelaide wouldn't have let that happen, unless the living Adelaide had dementia ... or they did it without telling her.

"Do you remember one of your ancestor Daisy in a blue dress?"

Josie thought for a minute. "Now that you mention it, I do. Mother liked that one especially, but it was at the top of the stairs and so gaudy. We took it down with the others after she ... umm ... passed."

"What happened to them? You didn't throw them out, did you?" I asked.

"Oh, no. We couldn't bring ourselves to do that. Someone in the family said they would find a home for them."

My blood chilled as I remembered Lisa saying she was selling things off to Felicity Bates. Felicity might already have the spell book in her possession, and that would be bad. Very bad.

"Who was it? Lisa?"

Josie made a face. "No, we wouldn't trust anything to her. It wasn't Lisa. It was Max."

Chapter 23

By the time I left the Hamiltons', my head was spinning. If Josie didn't kill Adelaide, then who did? Evie's behavior and odd demeanor put her at the top of my list. Josie had said she'd heard the squeaking of the dumbwaiter, which made me wonder if someone snuck up in there and killed Adelaide. That ruled out Evie and Julie, though, since all they had to do was walk down the hall. But someone who didn't want to be seen passing Evie, Julie, or Josie's rooms might have used it. Someone whose room wasn't in that hall but still had access to the house. Max? Lisa? John?

Josie said they'd given the paintings to Max. Did Max want the paintings because he knew the book was in one of them, or was he just trying to protect them from Lisa and make sure they stayed in the family, as he'd told Striker and me the night we were in the cottage? And if so, what did he do with them? They weren't in the cottage.

I had to admit that I liked Max, but I couldn't let that cloud my judgment. He'd seemed pretty upset that first night when he caught me digging in the daisy field. Had he buried the book there in the time capsule?

He'd seemed sincerely upset about Adelaide's death when he came to the bookstore to tell me that Josie had lied about being in the house that morning, but maybe it was all a ploy to cast suspicion away from him. He knew I was friends with Striker—maybe he thought I'd tell the police and they wouldn't look at him as a suspect.

My eyes fell on the cottage as I pulled out of the Hamilton driveway. I needed to go talk to Max. But if he was the killer, that could be dangerous. Though that had never stopped me before, and I couldn't call Striker or Gus because I didn't have a reason to suspect Max of Adelaide's death other than the fact that he might have killed her for the spell book. And I certainly couldn't tell them about *that*.

I pulled out onto the road and then drove up to the dirt road that ran behind the cottage. I parked my Jeep right at the cottage this time. If I disappeared, maybe someone would remember seeing it there. I walked right up to the door and knocked.

No answer.

I peeked in the window, cupping my hands over my eyes. The red and green lights on the equipment blinked, but the screen savers on the monitors were up. No one had used the computers in a while, and there was no sign of Max.

"Looking for someone?"

I spun around, and Julie was standing behind me, a pie plate with a blue-checkered cloth over it in her hand.

"I was looking for Max."

She frowned. "Oh, he's not home?"

"No." My eyes were still on the pie. "Did you bring that from your house?"

She glanced back at the mansion. "Yes. Cook made it, and I thought I'd run it over. It's blueberry. His favorite. What did you want? Maybe I can help you."

I studied Julie for a second. The rest of the Hamiltons had regarded me with suspicion from the get-go, but Julie didn't seem suspicious of me at all. Maybe I could get some information out of her. "Max and I have been working on something together, and I was wondering if there was a place he might store things that were precious to him. You know, like a hiding place. I was supposed to pick something up ..."

She gnawed on her bottom lip. "The only place I know of is the time capsule, but he wouldn't put anything in there until the ceremony." Julie pointed to the spot in the daisy field where the earth had been disturbed.

"Yeah, he told me about that. What is the ceremony?"

Julie shrugged. "My grandma started it a long time ago. We all put stuff in there. Every year we have a ceremony and put in some memorabilia for future generations."

"How big is it?"

"Oh, about this big." Julie balanced the pie plate as she spread her hands apart to indicate a container about three feet by four feet. Big enough to fit a book or even a small painting.

"When was the last time you guys buried something in it?" I asked.

"We do it every year on September fifteen." Julie looked at me curiously.

"Interesting." It was June, and judging by the way the ground was disturbed, someone had put something in there recently, not last September. I flicked my gaze back to Julie. "Do you know when Max will be back?"

She shook her head. "I actually thought he would be here, but you know Max. He comes and goes."

"Right. Well, thanks a lot." I wanted to rush over to the time capsule and start digging, but I couldn't do that in broad daylight with Julie watching, so I forced myself to walk back to the car. As I drove off, I craned my neck to look at the daisy field. Something had been buried there. Was it the spell book?

If it was, and Max was the killer, it might not be safe to come back and dig around there at night by myself. But if Max did kill Adelaide for the spell book, then why bury it in the time capsule? Surely he would want to use it right away or keep it handy...unless he was trying to keep it from falling into the wrong hands. Maybe Max didn't kill Adelaide but knew the power of the book. Once Adelaide was gone, he buried it to keep it safe. From whom? Evie?

There were a lot of what-ifs running around in my head, but one thing I knew for sure—I had to find out what Max was up to.

***

I called Max's cell phone and left a message for him to return the call. It might have been my worst mistake ever, but I mentioned the digging I'd seen near the time capsule. He might have one of his surveillance cameras pointed at it and might have caught someone burying something there. I had a gut feeling that Max was a good guy and, if I was right, he might be able to help. But if he was on the *other* side, he would know I was onto him, and that might not be good for my health. I shuddered to think of the harmful spells that might be inside that book. Spells he could use on *me*.

I rustled around the shop nervously. I called out to Adelaide, but she didn't show. Robert and Franklin popped in to discuss the weather, but they hadn't seen even a whisper of mist from her.

Even Pandora was restless, pacing back and forth and jumping in and out of her cat bed. Her constant meowing grated on my nerves, and I finally dug out her catnip toy to quiet her down. The end of the day came, and Max never returned my call. What was he doing all day? Did he have the spell book? And where were the paintings?

I decided I had no choice but to go back to the cottage and dig up that time capsule. I couldn't do that until later in the night if I had any hopes of not getting caught. I debated calling Striker to bring him with me for protection, but what would I tell him? I could say that I'd gotten a lead that some evidence was buried in the time capsule, but I didn't want to have to explain *how* I'd gotten such a lead. Probably better to go on my own.

Five minutes before closing, Pandora raced to the back door and paced back and forth until I closed up. She stared out the Jeep's side window all the way home, and when I pulled into the driveway and opened my door, she shot out of the car like a bullet and ran over to the path that led to Elspeth's house. Was she trying to tell me something? I hadn't checked in on Elspeth in a few days. It couldn't hurt to go over and see if she was okay while I was killing time before my excursion later that night.

I dropped my purse on the porch and followed Pandora. The smell of molasses cookies grabbed me halfway down the path and dragged me toward Elspeth's. My mouth was watering by the time I got there. Pandora veered toward the barn, and I toward the rose-laden porch. I could see into the house through the green wooden screen door with its scrolled corners. I knocked on the wooden frame of the screen door, and Elspeth yelled at me to come in. She was in the kitchen, scraping ginger-brown cookies off a cookie sheet onto a blue-and-white-flowered plate with a spatula.

"Would you like some cookies? This is one of your grandmother's recipes." Elspeth waved the cookie plate under my nose, and my mouth watered. I grabbed two and sat at the table.

Elspeth busied herself pouring tea. "Speaking of recipes. Did you ever find Adelaide's recipe book?"

"No. The Hamiltons are an odd bunch. I didn't see it in the cottage. Do you know of any other places Adelaide might store things she treasured?"

"No, dear. Sorry."

Disappointment settled on me, and I consoled myself by scarfing down another cookie. I knew the book was in the painting, but what had Max done with the painting? Could I trust him, or was he a killer?

"Do you know anything about Adelaide's grandson, Max?" I asked.

Elspeth's white brows tugged together. "Not much. Why do you ask about him?"

I shrugged. "I've met him a few times in the course of looking for the book, and he seems a little odd. He was using the cottage where Adelaide stored some of the family heirlooms, but now there's nothing in there. I just wondered if that recipe book—"

"Oh, I think I know what he did with those. In fact, I saw Max just this afternoon with a bunch of family portraits. I'm not sure if he had any other family heirlooms, though, and I didn't see any books." Elspeth's keen blue eyes studied me over the rim of her teacup.

"You saw him? Where?"

"The historical society. You know that lovely new building they've finally finished? They have a lot more room for displays in the museum now, and he was donating some of their things for future exhibits. Adelaide was a huge supporter of the society, and you know if you loan stuff to the historical society for them to put on display, the family retains possession."

My conversation with Max came back to me when he said he wanted to help his grandmother make sure some of the things remained part of the family. Was he merely helping out with the paintings and didn't even know about the spell book? And if so, was the painting of Daisy Hamilton in the blue dress at the historical society right now?

There was only one way to find out.

***

Pandora was filled with self-importance as she sat in the beam of light in the middle of Elspeth's barn. The other cats had gathered around her to listen to her tale of seeing the two ghosts, and a murmur of meows had circulated the barn when she'd told them she'd discovered, through the ghosts, that the book was in the old painting of Daisy Hamilton. Pandora was one of the very rare cats that could see and talk to ghosts, and she took great pride whenever she could use that ability to help Mystic Notch.

"And furthermore, I may have narrowed down who the evil foe is within the Hamilton ranks," Pandora said.

"How did you do that?" Ivy asked.

"I went on a foray to the Hamilton mausoleum with my human, and we ran into one of them inside. I sensed great evil."

"But who is it?" Otis said impatiently. *"Get on with that so we know who to avoid."*

"The dark twin, Evie. She's been very suspicious as well as unwelcoming. I felt her watching us from the patio the other night when we were at the Hamilton house trying to home in on the location of the book."

"Is she the only one?" Sasha asked. *"There may be more than one person there working against us. I believe I sensed an abundance of wicked thoughts at the house."*

Pandora's whiskers twitched. She was sure she'd felt something out of the ordinary from Evie, but she'd also sensed another presence at the house. *"We followed the daughter, Josie, out there, but I did not get a strong sense from her. Evie was with the young man, Brian, at first, but he disappeared quickly. Evie stayed in the mausoleum to threaten Willa. Evie was outside the house the other night when we were all there. We sensed evil intentions then as well."*

Inkspot tilted his head. "We'll take that into consideration. Everyone must be on alert around the Hamilton humans. But we still do not know where the painting is, so I don't see how we can take action."

"The book may not even be in the painting anymore," Kitty pointed out.

"True, but the painting is our only lead," Inkspot said.

"The information is worthless if we don't know where the painting is," Otis hissed.

A noise came from the area near the door, and they all turned to see two cats silhouetted in the light. One of them Pandora recognized as Alley, the three-legged cat. He was not part of Elspeth's barn clan but one of the many who helped them from time to time. Alley was one of the lucky ones —his human had actually driven for five hours to rescue him. Some cats and humans are just meant to be together.

"I've brought someone who may help," Alley said. Beside him, a large cat crouched on his haunches.

"Come forward," Inkspot demanded.

Alley stepped inside. Without the light at his back, Pandora could see the splash of white on his chest. The cat that was with him became more visible too. His deep golden eyes stared at them unblinkingly from a coat of jet-black fur. Something in his countenance was familiar, and Pandora stepped forward to sniff him.

"What is this information?" Snowball asked.

"This is Obsidian," Alley said. "Tell them what you told me."

Obsidian puffed up his chest, obviously unintimidated by the magical cats who were all now staring at him. "I am from a long line of felines who have been tasked with guarding Mystic Notch history...among other things. I dwell in and around the historical society building. Nothing escapes me. Today, there was a disturbance in the air. As you know, the humans form emotional attachments to material things. Today many of these things were donated, and I felt the pull of emotions, but along with that, I sensed an object of vital importance. Magical importance."

Kelley slid her green eyes at him. "What were these things?"

"Old family portraits."

The cats gasped. But Inkspot was old and wise, and Obsidian was unknown to the cats...or at least to most of them. Inkspot knew not to take anything at face value without verifying the source.

"How do we know what you say is true and not some sort of a trap?" Inkspot asked.

"That's right. You could be in cahoots with Fluff. This could be a way to lure us into Fluff's clutches," Sasha said.

Obsidian shrugged and started toward the door. "Suit yourselves."

"Wait!" Pandora spoke up. "I can vouch for Obsidian. I know of Obsidian's line. I've spoken to the ghost of his ancestor."

Obsidian stopped and turned to look at Pandora, his golden eyes softening. "You have?"

"Yes. The Obsidian whose human was Hester Warren. I had reason to communicate with him some months ago. Nice fellow," Pandora said.

"He is well?" The tone of Obsidian's question made clear his loyalty to and care for his ancestors.

"Yes," Pandora answered.

Inkspot studied Pandora carefully. "The ghost cat you communicated with earlier is one of his kin?"

"Yes. I sniffed him, and he is blood lineage."

Inkspot glanced at Obsidian. "And we can trust his information?"

"I believe so. Besides, what else are we to do? If we bring enough cats and it is a trap from Fluff, we will overpower him."

"We have little choice. But there is power in numbers." Inkspot turned to Alley. "Will you

gather as many of the Mystic Notch cats as will help and bring them to the historical society?"

"Of course." Though Alley only had three legs, Pandora knew he could still run like the wind and would quickly be able to gather cats from all over Mystic Notch.

"I will stay with you and help as well," Obsidian said. "I know many entrances and escape routes of the building. That knowledge may come in handy."

"Very well." Obsidian looked around the room at the cats who had migrated out from every corner and behind every bale of hay to stand and were now swishing their tails, showing their eagerness to get started. "Let's all be on high alert. This mission is critical ... it could be a matter of life and death for Mystic Notch!"

Chapter 24

I bid Elspeth a hasty farewell and rushed outside, calling for Pandora. She was nowhere to be found, and I didn't have time to wait for her. Once the historical society people started looking at that painting, they might discover the spell book, and then what would happen to it? Besides, I knew my cat could take care of herself.

I rushed down the path up to my Jeep and drove toward town, my brain busy working on coming up with an excuse to be able to inspect the Hamilton paintings.

I'd graduated with Deb Hawkins down at the historical society, but would she let me look at the Hamilton paintings? I doubted it. I was certain she wouldn't let me rip one apart to see if a book was hidden behind the canvas, but how was I going to get my hands on the painting to even see if the book was in there?

As I turned into the parking lot, I realized I had a worse problem than that. It was seven at night. The historical society was closed.

My hands clenched the steering wheel as I contemplated my next move. I couldn't very well break in, could I? Could I call Striker and get him to use his police power to gain entrance? But what would I tell him? It would have to be some sort of emergency...

Movement on the side of the building caught my eye. My heartbeat kicked up a notch. Someone else was here. Were they looking for the spell book?

I hopped out of the Jeep and turned to close the door quietly. I didn't know if whoever was on the other side of the building was friend or foe, and if they were foe, I didn't want to alert them to my presence.

As I turned back, Marion came careening around the building, wheelchair squeaking in the night.

"Hurry! You must save the book. They've got it in the basement, but I can't get down the stairs in this wheelchair!" Marion knew about the book? Of course she did. She was Adelaide's twin sister. Had she been trying to protect it all this time? I didn't have much time to think about it, because she was shoving me toward the back of the building. "Be careful. The future of Mystic Notch hangs in the balance!"

The concrete stairs led down to the basement. A puddle of diffused yellow light illuminated the middle stairs but faded to dark toward the door, which was cracked open to reveal the dimly lit basement.

I crept down and pushed the door open a hair so I could slip in. I cocked my ear, listening for noise as my eyes adjusted to the lack of light. I had no idea what I was getting myself into. Who were the "they" that Marion was talking about? Maybe it wasn't so smart to rush down here—I was alone, and apparently there was more than one person with the book.

Somehow one of the Hamiltons must have found out the portraits were here. The *wrong* Hamilton. Marion had followed them here knowing that they were looking for the book. But who was it? I ruled out Max, because he would have already taken the book out of the painting instead of bringing it here. I wished I'd asked Marion more questions, but there hadn't been time.

Dark, hulking shadows of the stored items took shape, and I crept forward, being careful not to knock something over. A murmur of voices drifted out from the north corner. I moved in that direction.

"On hair of toad and light of moon ..." a young woman's voice chanted. Evie? I couldn't be sure who it was, but I was pretty sure I had zeroed in on *where* it was coming from. I wiggled through a thin opening in between two piles of boxes and ducked under something wrapped in a sheet then peeked out from behind a tall armoire.

Evie sat crouched in the corner. A black leather book about the size of a diary lay open in her lap. The gilding on the sides of the pages glinted in the dim light cast by the two bare bulbs that hung from the ceiling. Beside her, a painting was strewn against the wall. The canvas in one corner had been ripped, but the subject matter was evident—Daisy Hamilton in a blue silk gown.

My blood froze. Evie had the spell book and was using it to cast a spell.

Her eyes flicked up away from the book, and I shrank back. But her look wasn't aimed in my direction. It was aimed at something over to the right. Her accomplice—the other person Marion had mentioned.

How was I going to get the book away from two people?

But wait. Something wasn't right. If I wasn't mistaken, I could see the sheen of fear in her eyes. In fact, the way Evie was crouched down on the floor clutching the book, it almost looked as if she were cowering from something.

I shifted my position to try to see what that something was. The movement caught her eye. She saw me, her eyes widening in fear.

What the heck was going on?

"Give me the book, or I'll kill you." This voice was from a young male. Now it was clear. The two people weren't accomplices—they were enemies. Evie was obviously trying to protect the book from this person, but which one of them was the bad guy, and which one was the good guy?

"I'll never give this up! I'll turn you into a frog, and then you'll see who is stronger!" Evie focused back on the book, rocking back and forth as she chanted the spell.

The man snorted. "You wouldn't know how to cast a spell if you fell over one. You're too inexperienced. Now hand over the book so Mystic Notch can realize its full power."

It didn't really matter who was the good guy and who was the bad guy. I had to do something to get the book away from both of them. I looked around for a weapon. My movements caught Evie's attention again, and she glanced over nervously.

Unfortunately the gesture caught the attention of the other person. "What are you doing? Is someone over there?"

Shoot.

I stepped back, intending to squeeze between a stack of boxes and the wall to hide, but I caught my foot on the edge of a table and stumbled forward, shoving my arms out in front of me to stop from falling on my face. I rammed into a tower of cardboard boxes, which wobbled precariously. The top one fell, the cover flying off as it tumbled down. A river of clear crystal glasses spilled out and shattered all over the floor. Behind the box stood the person Evie had been battling with for the book. Julie's boyfriend, Brian.

He sneered at me. "It's the nosy bookseller. Figures."

He grabbed me by the arm so hard it felt as if it might snap out of the socket and hurled me across the room toward Evie.

Chapter 25

I slid across the broken glass, smashing head-first into the wall and landing on the floor beside Evie. She looked at me with wide eyes and clutched the book as if *I* were the one trying to take it.

"You can't have it!" She scrambled away from me, terrified. Did Evie think that *I* was the bad guy?

"Neither of you can have it," Brian bellowed. "Hand it over."

Evie flicked her eyes from me to Brian and then back to me. "You mean you aren't working together?"

I shook my head.

Evie's eyes narrowed. "But you were acting so suspicious."

"I was looking for the book to keep it safe."

"Too bad you didn't succeed," Brian said. "Neither of you did. So hand it over, or I can make things go really bad for both of you."

Evie shrank back and clutched the book even tighter. Her eyes flicked from Brian to the book. It was open, the yellowed page darkened and flaking on the edges. The faded writing looked like calligraphy type font.

"Distract him while I cast the spell. I think I can render him ineffective," Evie whispered.

My gaze drifted from Evie to Brian. It seemed obvious by the way he threw me into the wall that *he* was the bad guy. They seemed to be on opposite sides, so did that make Evie the good guy? I didn't know if I could trust either of them, but I didn't have much choice. Brian was advancing on us, his hand outstretched for the book. I decided to trust Evie.

Still crouched against the wall, the cold, hard cinderblocks against my back, I thrust my palms up in front of my face. "Wait a minute! You won't get away with this."

"Why not? When the two of you disappear, there won't be anyone to tell on me."

Brian glanced down at Evie, who was ignoring him as she read from the book, chanting words I couldn't quite understand.

"Don't bother with that," Brian said. "My magic is more powerful."

"So you were after the spell book all along?" I hoped the question would distract him and buy us some time for me to think of a way out. Brian stood between us and the basement door to the outside, but there had to be another door that led up into the museum. Brian had us backed into a corner, but if I could locate the other door, I might be able to do something to maneuver him out of the way so we could make a break for it.

"Is that why you killed Adelaide? For the book?" My question made Brian pause.

"Killed Adelaide? What are you talking about?"

Evie jerked her head up from the book. "You killed Gram? I knew you were up to something. I knew you never really had an interest in Julie, but if I thought you were a murderer, I would have done something drastic sooner. I just regret I couldn't make Julie see you for the jerk that you are."

"I didn't kill her. But I could have if I wanted to. Just like I can kill you if you don't do as I say." Brian reached into his pocket and pulled out a handful of something that looked like purple sand. He held his palm open, the tiny grains sparkling like gems. "I don't care what you think. All I want is the book, and if you know what is good for you, you'll hand it over right now." As if to prove his point, he hurled the sand in the direction of the door I'd come in through. It pelted the boxes, sheet-covered furniture, and floor.

There was a loud hissing sound.

The pungent smell of sulfur.

And then the boxes and furniture burst into flames.

So much for using *that* door to escape. Hopefully there was another exit around here somewhere. But where? I looked around frantically, trying to locate the top of a doorframe amidst the chaos of piled boxes, displays, and furniture. The only sources of light were two low-watt bulbs that hung from the ceiling and a thin sliver of moonlight that cut in from somewhere high on the wall to my left. It was too dim for me to see any doorways amongst the shadows.

Brian's lips curled into a grimace of a smile as he admired the fire, the flames lighting up the harsh angles of his face and reflecting in his eyes, giving him a maniacal look. Then he turned and took a step toward us.

I pushed myself up to a standing position just in case I needed to fight. I preferred to solve things with words and logic, but Brian didn't seem as if he were in the mood.

Evie was no help. She was still crouched on the floor, reading the book.

"Let us go, and I'll persuade Striker to go easy on you. Killing two more people will get you a life sentence, but since you only killed one person, you may not have to spend your *whole* life in jail."

Brian snorted. "Why do you keep saying that? I didn't kill anyone. My only crime is that I want that book, and as far as I know, nobody goes to jail for that. So hand it over, or I'll make sure your accident is incredibly painful."

"Don't lie. We know you killed Adelaide," I said.

"What? I didn't! Why would I? She didn't even remember where the book was. I thought *you* had it hidden. That's why I followed you around—even out to that creepy mausoleum. It was bad enough I had to pretend to like Julie so I could scour the house for it. That old bat was useless, but I didn't kill her."

I glance at Evie. If Brian didn't kill Adelaide, then who did? I couldn't worry about that now, though. The fire was growing stronger, and Brian was growing more desperate. We had to get out of there.

Evie still had her nose buried in the book. Her voice was barely above a whisper. I couldn't make out the words, which sounded like, "by wart of toad and silver light."

Silver light! The moonlight! I realized the light that was coming from the wall to my left must be from a window. A way out! I chanced a glance over and saw it out of the corner of my eye. It was narrow, only about two feet wide, and placed up over my head. Hope surged when I noticed the crank on the inside. If we could get over to it and crank it open, we could pile up some boxes and wriggle out...but in order to do that, we'd have to incapacitate Brian.

The flames licked higher over by the doorway. They'd spread to engulf the next pile of boxes. The knot in my stomach tightened as I searched around for some sort of weapon.

"Of webbed feet and wet domain, a toad will be thy name ... so mate it be!" Evie flung her hands out toward Brian, and we all stopped for a heartbeat. Nothing happened.

Brian laughed and stepped closer. I sidestepped to the right, feeling the corner of the walls on my back. There was a tall piece of furniture—a highboy—and something else beside it. Something with a long handle. I curled my fist around it and set my feet shoulder-width apart, bending my knees slightly so I would be ready to thrust the handle out in front of me and jab him where it would count the most.

Squeak. Squeak.

The three of us jerked our attention toward the window. Marion was out there in her wheelchair!

"You won't get away with it now," I said to Brian. "There's a witness out there."

Brian glanced at the window, and I took my chance. Rushing forward, I jabbed the long handle into his crotch with all my might.

"Oomph!" He doubled over and crashed to the floor.

"Evie, come on!" I rushed to the window and cranked it open. Fresh air spilled in, replacing the burning stench that had filled the room. From my vantage point below ground, all I could see were Marion's sensible-shoe-clad feet and the bottom of the chair's wheels. Then she bent down, her wrinkled face filling the window.

"Do you have the book?"

"Yes!" I glanced back nervously at Brian, who was rolling, curled in a fetal position, and moaning. I knew he wouldn't be incapacitated for long. We had to hurry!

"The book! Save the book! Hand it out first, and then I'll help you out!" Marion yelled.

Evie was on her feet, the book still open in her hands and still chanting. "On toadly form, so mate it be!" She flung her hands out at Brian again, but nothing happened.

"Forget about it, Evie. We don't have time! We have to get out now!" I grabbed the book from Evie and stood on my tiptoes to hand it out to Marion.

Her gnarled hand darted in and clamped onto the corner with a vise-like grip.

Something just behind the wheels of her chair caught my eye. Red stilettos.

Felicity Bates?

Why would Felicity be here helping us?

Marion tugged at the book just as I realized I'd made a huge mistake. Felicity wouldn't help us, and neither would Marion. It was a trap.

Marion tugged harder, and the book slipped out of my hand. She pulled it through the window then bent back down, looking in at us. "Sorry, Evie. I hate to do this to you, but it has to be done. By the way, it's 'so *mote* it be' ... Not '*mate*.' Stupid twit couldn't even get the spell jargon right," she muttered just before she slammed the metal storm covering over the outside of the window and locked it shut.

Chapter 26

"Now you've done it!" I whirled on the menacing voice to see Brian, now standing, his face red with rage. He spun around, whipping a nasty-looking sword whose blade was as wide as an airplane propeller off a black display board that had been hanging on the wall, and rushed toward us. The sword must have been part of a display. It looked three hundred years old. Hopefully it hadn't been sharpened since.

Evie whispered something, but I wasn't paying attention to her. I was busy thrusting my arms up over my face to keep Brian from slashing it with the sword. I braced myself for the pain.

"By form of toad, so mote it be!"

Splat.

The blow never came, and when I peeked out from behind my arms, sitting on the floor in front of us was a fat, ugly toad.

"It worked!" Evie's excitement was a little hard to understand, given our predicament.

I eyed the toad suspiciously. Had she actually just cast a spell? My grandmother's words to believe in magic came back to me. Did magic really exist? And if so, could we use it to escape?

"Great. Now make a spell to put that fire out so we can get out of here." I jerked my chin toward the fire, which was now consuming several boxes and working its way toward an old oak-and-glass display case. The temperature in the basement had gone up a few degrees, and beads of sweat formed on my forehead. To top it all off, my leg ached worse than it had in months.

Evie's face fell. "I don't actually know any spells. That's why I wanted the book."

"But you just turned Brian into a toad."

A smile ghosted across her lips as she glanced down at the toad, which glared up at her with its liquid-gold eyes. "Gram always said I was special, and I knew I had powers, but I never knew the words to unleash them." She glanced over toward the window, her smile fading. "And now I guess I still don't."

I didn't have time to commiserate with Evie. "We need to find the door out of here, pronto. Let's skirt the wall and see if we can locate it."

"Okay. I'm sorry I suspected you. I could tell you were after the book, and I knew I had to protect it. I didn't know from whom, though."

"Let's just focus on getting out of here." I could hardly blame her—I'd suspected *her* too.

I slipped through rows of boxes and wiggled behind tall chests and display cases, feeling my way around the dim basement, looking for a door in the wall. It was hard going—the basement was crammed with old displays, boxes of historical artifacts, and various donated items. The smell of burning wood and cardboard added to the urgency, each crackle of the flames ratcheting my anxiety to a higher level.

"There has to be a door up into the museum around here somewhere," I yelled. But the basement was big. Would we be able to cover the entire perimeter before the fire engulfed it?

"I can't believe Aunt Marion turned on me." Evie's voice shook as she pressed along the wall next to me. "No wonder she kept asking about the book. I think she thought Gram had told me where it was. I looked for it because she said she wanted to help me learn the spells, and the whole time I just played into her hands."

"I'm sorry about that, but you couldn't know she wanted the book for evil purposes."

Evie stopped and looked at me wide eyed. "Just what *is* she going to do with the spell book, anyway?"

"I don't know, but whatever it is, we aren't going to like it. We have to get out of here and stop her." *Because burning alive in here won't do anyone any good, least of all us.*

"The room is filling up with smoke. I can't even see the wall." Evie coughed. "Hey, what about Brian? He would have had to have known the other way out in order to escape!"

"Right. Too bad you turned him into a toad."

"His body is a toad, but his *mind* still thinks like Brian. If he knows a way out, he'll head there. Even a toad doesn't want to burn up."

We raced through the haze back to the spot where we'd been standing when Evie cast her spell. I could still see a wet oval blotch on the floor where the toad version of Brian had sat. Smaller wet marks led toward the southwest corner. We followed them, shoving boxes and furniture out of the way as the fire threatened behind us.

"Over here!" Evie had made it to the corner first and had shoved several boxes aside to reveal a large steel door. Relief flooded through me as I rushed over to it. I grabbed the doorknob and twisted, pulling the door. It didn't budge. I twisted in the other direction and pulled again, but to no avail.

The door was locked.

***

Pandora smelled the fire even before she saw the smoke billowing from the back of the historical society building. As they raced out of the woods, her worst fears were realized. The building was on fire, and Willa was inside!

Inkspot was in the lead. He stopped at the edge of the woods so the herd of cats would be hidden by the tall grass as they watched the goings-on in the parking lot. Pandora could see things were not going well. The old lady, Marion, sat in her wheelchair near a long black sedan. If that wasn't enough to raise Pandora's suspicions, the person standing in front of Marion was. It was Felicity Bates, and she didn't look happy. The cats watched as she bent down, trying to snatch the book out of Marion's clutches. Marion pulled back, and the two ladies got into a noisy tug-of-war punctuated by the squeaking of Marion's wheelchair wheels as she was pulled forward and pushed back.

"That's the spell book! I can sense it," Squeaky, a tiger cat who was one of the lucky feral cats that found a forever home, whispered from beside Pandora.

But Pandora was too distracted by the plumes of smoke coming out of the basement door of the building to worry about the book.

"I'm going in." Pandora started to spring toward the building, but Otis shot out his paw and held her back.

"Patience, little one. We cannot rush in," Otis said.

"My human is in there. I must save her!"

"Don't worry. We will. But we must be strategic," Otis assured her.

"Is Fluff here with the red-haired witch?" Woodson, a tall buff tabby, asked.

The cats hunkered down, all of them dialing up their senses in search of Fluff. Pandora did not catch even the slightest whiff of the offensive cat. Remembering the conversation she'd had with him in the bookstore window, she was not surprised.

"Fluff is not here," she said. "He has trained his human to do the work for him, so he doesn't need to get his claws dirty. He is likely at home, snoozing on a silk pillow."

"Spoiled rotten," Kelley said.

"They're getting away! We must hurry!" Olive's light-blue eyes registered alarm. Pandora tore her gaze from the burning building and looked over at the two women. Marion had pro-

duced a silver-handled cane and was beating Felicity off as she tried to maneuver herself into the sedan.

"We must stop them. All cats converge on the woman with the book. Do not let her get away!" Inkspot commanded then turned to Pandora. "Pandora, take Otis and Obsidian into the museum and save Willa."

Pandora didn't need to be told twice. She was already up and racing toward the building before Inkspot had finished the sentence.

"This way." Obsidian took the lead. "The basement door is blocked by the fire. Too dangerous. But I know of a secret entrance."

Pandora's heart twisted as they raced toward the building. It had taken her a long time to get Willa to the mediocre state of understanding they had between them now, but she had to admit she'd grown quite attached to the human. The thought of life without her was unbearable.

Pandora glanced at Otis running by her side, his face focused on the task ahead, concentrating on saving the humans. She felt a rush of camaraderie. She knew that despite their differences, she could count on the persnickety calico.

Obsidian led them to one of the basement windows. It was shuttered with a metal shutter, but there was a small opening in one corner, and they squeezed through, plopping down onto the cold concrete below. Pandora already had her senses amped up, and she could easily see the hulking furnace and ductwork despite the fact that it was pitch black in the furnace room. Her sense of smell was also heightened, and her whiskers twitched at the smells of burning cloth and wood as well as melting rubber and plastic.

"We must find Willa before the fire gets her." Pandora lifted her nose to the air, trying to scent her human. Her gut churned. Willa could be lying unconscious anywhere in the basement of the large building. How would she find her? All she could smell was smoke.

"I know of the display that holds items you can use to squelch the fire," Obsidian said as he padded quickly toward the door that opened into the rest of the basement. "You must lead your human to the items so she can use them properly. It is not something cats can do easily."

"Fine. Fine," Otis said. "Let's get a move on. We don't have much time."

Obsidian snaked his paw under the crack in the door and pulled it open then slipped out, with Otis and Pandora following. The basement was thick with smoke. Panic shot through Pandora. Were they on time? Where was Obsidian taking them? She wondered if it was a wild goose chase, if there was really some display that could stop the fire, and if so, would Willa even know how to use it?

Obsidian stopped at a pile of boxes. He jumped up on something next to them and peered down, his claw reaching out and snagging the corner of the box and flipping the flaps open. Otis and Pandora joined him and peered into the box. Inside were several glass balls filled with some sort of liquid. There were red balls and clear balls. Pandora's shoulders hunched in disappointment. There was not enough liquid to put out the fire that she could hear raging on the other end of the basement.

"Is this some kind of trick?" Otis looked at Obsidian skeptically. "How can these put out a fire?"

"These were found in the attic of the fire department. They are antique fire grenades with special liquid. You throw them at the fire, and they act like a fire extinguisher. Unfortunately, they must be thrown, and cats cannot do that." Obsidian looked at Pandora. "We must lead Willa to them."

Pandora didn't have much choice but to trust Obsidian. Not to mention that she didn't have any better ideas. "Okay, but first we must find her."

As if Willa had read Pandora's mind, her voice called out from the southwest corner of the room. "Help! Is anyone out there?"

The cats raced in that direction, darting out from behind an old display case to see Willa frantically pulling on the handle of a large metal door.

***

Striker sped down Main Street on his way toward the historical society building just outside of town. Was it a coincidence that Louis's ghost had popped up with a hunch that the item Adelaide hid the book in may have been donated to the society at the same time he received an anonymous call about a disturbance involving a gaggle of cats in the parking lot of that same building? He didn't think so.

"I just hope the book hasn't been discovered and thrown out as junk." Striker was afraid that if it had, the old man's ghost would haunt him forever.

He careened into the parking lot, his attention on the black sedan parked over by the building, beside which Marion Hamilton sat in her wheelchair, covered in cats. He'd envisioned a couple of alley cats tipping over a trash barrel, not a woman covered in a living-cat coat.

He parked facing the sedan and got out. "What's going on here?"

"Get these darn cats off me!" Marion beat at the cats with her hands and poked at them with her cane, but there were dozens of them, all clinging to her and purring. They were in her lap, on her shoulders, on her ankles, and intertwined in the spokes of the chair's wheels. There was even one on top of her head—a large black cat that stared at Striker with uncanny intelligence in its golden eyes.

"I'm sorry, ma'am. I don't know what is going on here. What are you doing in this parking lot after hours?" Striker tried to pull a seal-point Siamese off Marion's shoulder, but the cat hissed and struck out at him, causing him to jump back. What was the old lady doing here? The building had been closed for hours. What possible reason would she have to be here...unless she was also looking for the book?

"I just came out for a ride. I'm an old woman and shouldn't be subjected to this. Please get rid of these creatures."

The back door of the car was open. Marion had been trying to get in the backseat. But if she was getting in the back, that meant she wasn't the driver. "Who drove you here?"

"I drove her." Striker turned to see John, the Hamiltons' butler, at the edge of the woods, brushing leaves and debris from his black suit.

Striker looked over John's shoulder into the woods. "What were you doing in the woods?"

"I was chasing after Fel... er ... I mean, I had a call of nature."

Striker knew enough to know the man was lying, but he didn't have a chance to interrogate him, because just then a loud crack from the building stole his attention. He whirled around to see plumes of smoke coming from the back. The building was on fire! He swiveled back to look at Marion and John. "Did you set the building on fire?"

John's eyes were wide. He looked just as surprised to see the building on fire as Striker. "No. I had nothing to do with that, but there are two people in there."

"How do you know? What people?" An uneasy feeling settled in Striker's chest.

John's eyes drifted to the other end of the parking lot. Striker hadn't thought to look down there when he'd driven in—his attention had been on Marion and all the cats. He followed John's gaze, his heart twisting when he recognized Willa's Jeep.

"I'm not sure if they are still in there, but I believe that nosy bookseller woman, Brian, and Evie Hamilton are inside."

Striker didn't wait for him to finish. He was off and running toward the building as soon as he'd seen Willa's Jeep. Sirens wailed in the distance. Someone had called the fire department, but Striker couldn't wait for them to arrive. He rushed toward the burning building and prayed that it wasn't too late.

Chapter 27

"It's locked!" I released the knob and pounded on the door. "Help! Is anyone up there?"

Evie collapsed against the door. "There's no one up there, Willa. The museum is closed."

I spun around and eyed the growing fire. There was no way we could get through it to the basement door, so I would have to find either another door or a way to put the fire out.

"The toad escaped through here." Evie pointed to a wet splotch under the door. "Now I wish I had never cast that spell."

"Why? Seemed like that was smart. He was going to cut us up with a sword." I looked around the perimeter for the signs of another door ... or maybe a fire extinguisher.

"Brian killed Gram, and I want him to pay. But unless I can turn him back from a toad, that's not going to happen."

"Won't happen if we burn up in a fire, either," I said. "But anyway, I don't think it was Brian who killed her. He seemed to be telling the truth when he said he didn't."

Evie screwed up her face. "Well, then who killed her?"

"I hate to tell you, but I think it was Marion... and I think I know how to prove it if we can just get out of here." It made perfect sense now. Marion wanted the spell book and probably killed Adelaide in an attempt to get her sister to tell her where it was, or to get her out of the way so she could search for it. Marion didn't have a lot of time left herself, so she wouldn't want to wait around for Adelaide to die of natural causes. The squeaking Josie had heard in the hall that morning wasn't someone sneaking up through the dumbwaiter—it was Marion's wheelchair. I'd noticed tracks near the disturbed earth the first time I'd gone to the daisy field. I'd thought it was someone digging for the spell book, but what if it was Marion hiding evidence? She knew they only opened the time capsule once a year and only to put stuff *in*. If she'd killed Adelaide and had buried the evidence underneath everything else in there, the chances were no one would find it for a hundred years.

Evie's eyes misted. "No. I thought Aunt Marion was..." Her voice drifted off, and she glanced at the window that Marion had slammed to bar our escape. "Well, I guess she wasn't what I thought she was."

"Meow!"

My blood froze. Was I hearing things?

"Did you hear a cat?" Evie asked.

"How could there be a cat in here? We would have heard it before, wouldn't we?" I vaguely remembered something about the historical society museum having a resident cat. Maybe it had been napping down here and was now trapped in the basement with us. If that were the case, I would have to find it. I couldn't escape and leave the cat to burn in the fire.

"We have to find it!" Evie echoed my thoughts as she looked around frantically.

"Meow!"

I squinted in the direction of the sound. Visibility inside the basement was waning, but I thought I saw the shape of a cat. And then they materialized out of the gloom. Not just one cat, but three...and one of them looked very familiar.

"Pandora?"

"Meow."

Pandora trotted over to me and rubbed her cheek against my ankle. How had she gotten in here? The last time I'd seen her, she was at Elspeth's, and that was several miles from here. Had she followed me? I bent down to pet her silky ears, my heart twisting at the thought of Pandora burning up in the fire. Not to mention the thought of *me* burning up in it.

But if Pandora had found a way to get in, maybe we could use that same path to get out.

"*Merooomee.*" Pandora nipped at my ankle and then trotted off toward a stack of boxes.

"No! Pandora, stay here!" I didn't want her disappearing into the bowels of the basement, where I wouldn't be able to find her.

She turned and flipped her tail at me, the kinked end pointing toward the pile of boxes she'd been aiming for.

"I think she's trying to tell you something," Evie said.

The other two cats, one of them a large black cat, the other an orange calico that I thought I'd seen at Elspeth's before, trotted over to the boxes, each of them meowing and rubbing their faces against the bottom box. I could see the top box had been clawed open. *Was* Pandora trying to tell me something? She did seem to be much more perceptive than other cats, and if there was ever a time to believe that Pandora was more than just an ordinary house cat, now was that time.

I headed over to the boxes, took the top one from the pile, placed it on the floor, and pulled the flaps open wide. Evie looked in over my shoulder.

"It's just a bunch of glass balls." Her voice dripped with disappointment.

She started to walk off, but I grabbed her arm. "Wait a minute. These aren't just glass balls." In my hunt for antique books, I attended estate sales and antique auctions on a regular basis and was quite familiar with all kinds of unusual antiques. That's how I knew these were not just glass balls filled with water—they were fire grenades, the old-fashioned version of a fire extinguisher. They were good at putting out fires, and twelve of them were nestled inside the box. I glanced back at the fire, which had spread to encompass the entire corner of the basement. Would twelve be enough?

I turned to Evie. "These are antique fire grenades. They were old-fashioned fire extinguishers. But I'm not sure they'll be enough. Can you do a spell to make them more potent?"

Evie's eyes widened. "Spell? No. I've never been any good at spells. Not without the book."

"But surely it can't hurt to try? You must remember something..."

She glanced down into the box uncertainly. A flicker of emotions ran across her face. The cats sat stock-still, staring up at us, their tails swishing on the basement floor. My heartbeat ticked away each precious second. We didn't have any time to lose.

"Okay. I'll try it."

She stepped closer to the box and shut her eyes tight. Waving her hands over the balls, she chanted.

"Within these balls, I summon the power
Triple their strength for our need of the hour
Fight the fire and save our souls
Let nature take course, so mote it be."

Evie stepped back, looked at me, and shrugged. "I don't know if it worked."

Pandora meowed and nudged my ankle as if telling me to go for it.

I picked up the box and headed to the corner where the fire was. "Come on. Let's go find out!"

Evie hurried behind me. When I got close enough, I set the box down and grabbed two of the grenades. "Grab one in each hand, and throw it at the base of the fire as hard as you can."

She grabbed one, and we pulled our arms back at the same time.

"Ready?" I looked at her, and she nodded. I glanced behind me to make sure the cats were at a safe distance. They stood in a row, staring at us intently. "Okay. One. Two. Three. Throw!"

Four balls hurled toward the base of the fire. They smashed on the ground, the liquid spreading out, eating into the orange flames, which hissed and sputtered in protest. The fire receded a few feet. Either Evie's spell had worked, or these things did a lot better job than I'd anticipated.

"It's working! I think my spell worked!" Evie grabbed two more balls, as did I.

"Let's focus on the area near the door. We might be able to beat the fire back enough to create an opening we can run out through."

We skirted to the left and raised the balls.

"Ready?" I asked.

Evie nodded.

"One. Two. Three. Throw!"

The balls smashed in the edge of the fire, resulting in a cloud of smoke and hissing steam. We covered our noses and mouths, waiting for the smoke to clear. When it did, my heart leapt—I could see the cellar door!

We had four more balls left, and if they worked as well as the others had, we'd be able to set the fire back enough to run through. "One more time!"

We picked up the balls and smashed them into the fire. It sputtered, the flames shooting high then dying back to the ground. "Let's go!"

Evie didn't need to be told twice. She took a deep breath and plunged through the thin wall of flames.

I glanced back at the cats. Would they follow, or would I have to pick them up and carry them out? I needn't have worried. The cats shot forward, diving through the fire, out into the night.

I turned and lurched after them just as a large body barreled through the opening and collided with me, knocking me back into the basement.

Chapter 28

"Striker?" I sputtered just as he caught me from falling on my butt.

"Chance! Thank God you're okay." The look of concern on his face melted my heart, but the flames jumping up behind him told me we didn't have time for a mushy reunion.

I turned him around and shoved him forward. "The fire!"

He put his arms around me, covering me to shield me from the flames, and we ran through the thin line of fire and spilled out into the night just as the firefighters were coming around the corner.

"In there!" Striker pointed down to the basement as if they needed direction. Flames were already coming out of the stairway.

I sucked in the first night air. Even though it still smelled of charred wood, it was refreshing. I bent over with my hands on my knees and coughed as my lungs got used to the clean air.

Striker grabbed my hand and turned me toward him. "Are you okay? What were you doing in there?"

"I'm fine. What are you doing here?" I straightened and glanced toward the parking lot.

"I got a strange call about her, and when I came I saw Marion surrounded by cats. I don't know what's going on—"

Cats! "I have to make sure Pandora is okay!" I broke free from Striker and ran around the building, looking for Pandora, stopping short when I got to the parking lot and saw Marion in her wheelchair, covered in cats.

Pandora was sitting on the ground in front of the chair. She looked at me and slit one eye shut, almost as if winking.

"Scat!" Marion batted at the tenacious felines, who seemed quite content to cling to her. Too bad the spell book was not in her lap or clutched in her hands. My stomach tightened. Where was the book? I looked around for Felicity. She was nowhere to be found, but I did notice deep divots in the ground, heading off to the woods. Stilettos? It looked as if Felicity had gotten away, but had she taken the book with her?

I didn't know what kind of deal Felicity had going with Marion, but I knew one thing—if Marion would sell out her own grand-niece, Evie, she'd likely have no qualms about double-crossing Felicity. I doubted she'd given her the book.

Maybe Marion had tossed the book in the car.

I ran around to the passenger side, opened the door, and poked my head in. It wasn't on the seat. Maybe underneath? I crouched down and tilted my head to look under the seat. Nothing. I lifted up the floor mat. Nothing. The door on the other side of the car opened, and I jerked my head up, meeting Striker's gray gaze over the hump in the middle of the car.

"Are you looking for something?" he asked.

"No. You?"

"Nuh-uh."

"Oh dear, this is quite a mess, now isn't it?" I pulled my head out of the car and spun around to face the owner of the familiar voice. "Elspeth?"

She stood next to the car, her eyes drifting over to the smoking building, then to Marion, then to me.

"Hello, dear. I hope you are not hurt." She looked me up and down, clutching a large patent-leather purse to her chest.

"No, I'm fine, but what are you doing here?"

"Oh. I heard about the fire on my scanner, and I rushed right down. You know some of Mystic Notch's most precious artifacts are in that building, waiting to be put in the new displays. I do hope nothing has been ruined." Her face looked agitated. She glanced over at Marion. "I didn't know Marion liked cats so much."

I followed her gaze. "I don't think she likes cats so much as ..."

"Evening, ma'am." John, the Hamiltons' butler, appeared seemingly out of nowhere. His outstretched hand held the leather spell book.

Elspeth's eyes dropped to the book. "Oh dear, is that Betty's old recipe book? I thought we lost that years ago." She took the book gently from John, who smiled at her.

"It was lost for a while, but now it is right where it should be," John said, then he turned to me and winked.

I wasn't sure what to say, but before I could open my mouth to speak, I was distracted by Evie, who was crouched down by the back tire of the car.

"Here, Toady." She lowered her head, peering under the tire.

"What are you doing, child?" Elspeth asked.

"Oh, there's a toad under here, and...I..."

"*Meow!*"

Leo, a beige Persian with long fur and a smooshed-in face and orange eyes, trotted over. Sneaking his paw under the tire, he swatted at the toad, giving it no choice but to hop out from its hiding place. Evie pounced on it, cupping it in her hands. She stood with a triumphant look on her face.

Elspeth had moved closer to watch her. "A pet toad? An unlikely pet for a girl like you. What are you going to do with him?"

Evie opened her cupped hands to look in at the toad. "I'm going to make sure he has the life that he deserves."

Elspeth nodded as if understanding exactly what Evie meant.

"You look like a young girl that would be interested in cooking." Elspeth held the book up. Evie's eyes widened, and she nearly dropped the toad.

Elspeth slipped a thin arm around Evie's shoulders, leading her away from the car. "Maybe I could teach you how to make some of these recipes the right way."

"That sounds lovely," Evie said.

I slid a look at Striker. Did he think it was odd that Evie had a toad or that John had given Elspeth a book that she was now going to use to teach Evie to cook while all the time, the building was on fire and Marion was draped in cats?

He just watched them walk off, a bemused smile on his face.

"Figures I would find you here." My sister's voice interrupted my thoughts. Gus stood a few feet away, her arms crossed over the chest of her khaki sheriff shirt. "Did you have something to do with this fire?" She gestured toward the building.

"No. Of course not," I said.

Her eyes raked me from head to toe, and I realized I was probably covered in soot, and I was pretty sure my hair was sticking out all over the place.

"You look like you had something to do with it," she said.

"Well, I was *in* it. I didn't *set* it."

"What were you doing in there? Were you following Marion to investigate Adelaide's death?" Her eyes flicked over to where Marion was, and I realized the cats had all dispersed and one of Gus's deputies was attempting to put Marion in handcuffs.

"No, I wasn't actually following her...you're arresting her?"

Gus snorted. "Come on, I know you've been investigating. In fact, I suspect you were responsible for the anonymous tip that led us to Marion."

"Tip?"

"Don't play dumb with me. The time capsule. We found the evidence buried inside."

My brows tugged together. I hadn't had time to call in a tip about my suspicions that Marion buried something in the time capsule, so who had called it in? Max? Maybe he saw Marion on one of his surveillance tapes and decided to turn her in. I knew he'd watched the tapes from the morning of Adelaide's death, but he probably hadn't looked at any after that. And given the time of death and when Marion pretended to discover Adelaide, she wouldn't have had time that morning. Plus she'd have wanted to wait until dark. Which meant she probably snuck out that night. I'd probably never know if Max had called that in, but it didn't matter as long as justice was done.

"I wasn't exactly sure it was in there, but I knew Marion had been out to the time capsule, and I just put two and two together." I shrugged.

Gus frowned. "How did you even know there *was* a time capsule? You seem to have a way of getting these suspects to open up and spill their guts. Maybe I should consider hiring you to help with investigations."

My brows shot up. That could be fun. "Really?"

Gus laughed. "No."

"Oh." I tried to hide my disappointment.

"Why would I spend money hiring you when you already do it for free?" she added.

Was she giving me the okay to meddle in investigations? It was hard to say, knowing her. "So what was in the time capsule anyway?"

"Adelaide's pillowcase. We think Marion suffocated her, and if that's true, we'll find epithelial cells and saliva from Adelaide on one side of the pillow and cells from Marion on the other."

That was why Adelaide's pillowcases didn't match when Josie found her that morning. Marion had taken the case off the pillow she'd used to suffocate her.

A loud shout came from the deputy trying to cuff Marion, and Gus glanced over. "Excuse me. Looks like I need to go help out over there."

She stormed off toward Marion, who was beating at the deputy with her cane. Marion was not going in without a fight. Sad that she would kill her twin sister. My heart crunched for Evie, who had trusted Marion. I got the impression the young girl thought of Marion as a mentor.

But maybe Evie had a new mentor now. Across the parking lot, Evie and Elspeth stood shoulder to shoulder. Their heads were bent together conspiratorially over the book. As I watched, Evie brought her cupped hands up and opened them a crack. Elspeth poked a finger in at the toad, and the two of them laughed. Maybe Elspeth would ensure Brian got just what he deserved.

Everything might just be okay in the end.

I glanced at Striker. Maybe everything would be okay for everyone else, but what about Striker and me?

Striker might have been thinking along the same lines, because he stepped closer and tucked a lock of flyaway hair behind my ear.

"Maybe now that this business is all over, we can pick up where we left off." His eyes flicked from mine to something behind my left shoulder, and his brows tugged together slightly.

"That would be nice," I said as a misty form appeared behind his shoulder.

"Yes, you can get back to your young man now. Because of you, I've reunited with my true love, Louis," Adelaide said.

"Finally," I replied out loud.

"Well, it hasn't been *that* long," Striker said.

"What? Oh, I didn't mean that."

"What did you mean?"

"Nothing. Everything is going to end up just perfect." My attention drifted from Striker to Adelaide, who mouthed the words "thank you" then puckered up and turned to kiss the empty space beside her as she slowly faded away.

***

Striker gave Louis's ghost a slight nod then raised a brow in a silent gesture for the old guy to be on his way. The book had been found. Louis had never said what to do with the book, but the fact that Elspeth had it in her possession *felt* right. He still wondered what the fuss over a recipe book was but was learning that there were many mysteries in Mystic Notch that defied reason.

"Now that the book is where it should be, I'll leave you to your earthly pursuits. Don't forget, son, once you find the right woman, she's worth waiting decades for." Louis waggled his brows at Striker and then puckered up and turned to kiss what appeared to be thin air.

Weird thing to do, Striker thought. But then who could make sense of ghosts, anyway?

"She sure is," Striker said out loud.

"She sure is what?" Willa asked.

Striker flicked his gaze from the quickly vanishing Louis to Willa. His chest tightened at the strange look she was giving him. Had he said that out loud? He'd have to watch himself around Willa if any more ghosts appeared. He didn't want to scare her off.

"She ... err ... *you* sure are *welcome* to invite me over for dinner any time you want now," Striker said.

"Oh. Well, you have been working a lot of hours lately, and I wasn't sure if you'd have time for dinner with me..."

"That's done with now. I'm going to have a lot more free time." Striker looked up again just to reassure himself that Louis was actually gone then stepped closer to Willa, cupped her chin with his hand, and pressed a kiss on her lips.

"Then I can't think of any better time to start picking up where we left off than right now." Willa stood on her tiptoes and kissed him back.

***

Pandora watched Willa and Striker kiss with mixed feelings of happiness and disdain. She was glad to see the two of them resuming their romance, but she found the human habit of touching lips to be disgusting. Pandora was thankful Elspeth had the book, and it looked as if she was going to pass along some knowledge to Evie. Pandora's chest tightened at the mistake she'd almost made. When she'd sensed evil in the mausoleum, it hadn't been Evie as she'd assumed...it had been Brian. Luckily Brian was now in a form that could harm no one. She'd have to take care next time not to jump to conclusions.

"All's well that ends well," Otis said as they walked toward the building, dodging the activities of the humans. The fire had been put out, and there was now a flurry of activity as they rolled up hoses and inspected the basement for damage. All the other cats had left. Inkspot and the others from Elspeth's gang had gone back to the barn. Only Obsidian, Pandora, and Otis remained behind to see it to the end.

"Not all is well. The historical society has been damaged," Pandora pointed out. "I hope your home is not ruined, Obsidian."

"Nah, the fire was contained in the basement. I never liked those displays that are stored near the door anyway. One is on wolves and canines of the White Mountains." Obsidian shivered. "Thankfully the important displays are still intact upstairs. Like the one from the early days of the notch, featuring Hester Warren and my ancestor."

"And the Egyptian display with the great cat god Bastet," Otis said.

"Yes," Obsidian agreed. "It would be a tragedy if anything happened to that. The humans need to view that more and learn how important our kind really is."

"Or maybe it's better they don't so we can fly under the radar," Otis said then added, "Hey, if

you need a place to stay, you can come back to Elspeth's barn with me. You will be most welcome."

Pandora suppressed a cat-like smile. "Otis, you better stop being so nice, or you'll ruin your reputation."

Otis scoffed. "Never you mind, little one. I still have plenty of grouchiness to go around."

They stopped in front of Willa's Jeep. "I'll wait here for my human. She'll worry about me if I run back on my own. Will you be okay to go back to the barn without me?" Pandora slid a glance at Otis.

Otis puffed his chest out. "Of course. Believe it or not, I have strong powers, though I choose only to use them when necessary."

Pandora turned to Obsidian. "Will you be okay in the museum tonight?"

"Yes, I have a cushy sleeping area in a nook upstairs, far from the fire. I will be fine."

"Very well, then. I suppose we should all part ways." Otis nodded at Pandora and then Obsidian. "'Til next time." Then he trotted across the asphalt and disappeared into the dark shadows of the woods.

"I thank you for your help, Obsidian." Pandora bowed to the big black cat.

"It's the least I could do for one who has talked to my ancestor." Obsidian paused and appraised her with his golden eyes. *"So the story is true—my ancestor guarded the box entrusted to his human even after his nine lives ran out."*

"Yes. He was a brave hero."

Obsidian's whiskers twitched proudly. *"I'm honored to share his name, then."* He glanced back at the parking lot. Gus had finally crammed Marion into the police car, the firefighters had reeled the hose back into the truck, and Willa and Striker were walking toward them, their hands clasped together. *"Looks like your human is almost ready to leave. I hope we meet again."*

"As do I." Pandora hopped up onto the hood of the Jeep to wait for Willa. She curled up into a ball, one eye on her human, the other closed tight. She was in dire need of a catnap. She'd barely slept in the past few days, preferring to remain awake to ensure that Fluff or his human didn't pull a fast one. But now, the book was safe, and Willa was one step closer to believing in magic. Pandora could finally rest, knowing that everything was right in Mystic Notch. At least for now.

The end.

About The Author

USA Today Bestselling author Leighann Dobbs has had a passion for reading since she was old enough to hold a book, but she didn't put pen to paper until much later in life. After a twenty-year career as a software engineer with a few side trips into selling antiques and making jewelry, she realized you can't make a living reading books, so she tried her hand at writing them and discovered she had a passion for that, too! She lives in New Hampshire with her husband, Bruce, their trusty Chihuahua mix, Mojo, and beautiful rescue cat, Kitty.

Find out about her latest books and how to get discounts on them by signing up at:
http://www.leighanndobbs.com/newsletter

If you want to receive a text message alert on your cell phone for new releases , text COZYMYSTERY to 88202 (sorry, this only works for US cell phones!)

Connect with Leighann on Facebook:
http://facebook.com/leighanndobbsbooks

More Books By Leighann Dobbs:

Mooseamuck Island
Cozy Mystery Series
* * *

A Zen For Murder
A Crabby Killer
A Treacherous Treasure

Mystic Notch
Cat Cozy Mystery Series
* * *

Ghostly Paws
A Spirited Tail
A Mew To A Kill
Paws and Effect

Blackmoore Sisters
Cozy Mystery Series
* * *

Dead Wrong
Dead & Buried
Dead Tide
Buried Secrets

Deadly Intentions
A Grave Mistake
Spell Found

Lexy Baker
Cozy Mystery Series
* * *

Killer Cupcakes
Dying For Danish
Murder, Money and Marzipan
3 Bodies and a Biscotti
Brownies, Bodies & Bad Guys
Bake, Battle & Roll
Wedded Blintz
Scones, Skulls & Scams
Ice Cream Murder
Mummified Meringues
Brutal Brulee (Novella)

Printed in Great Britain
by Amazon